For Crosby

J. NATHAN

This book is a work of fiction. Names, characters, places, and incidents are the product of the author's imagination or are used fictitiously and are not considered to be real. Any resemblance to actual events, locales, or persons, living or dead, is coincidental.

Edited by Stephanie Elliot

Cover Design by Letitia at RBA Designs
Cover Photo by Lindee Robinson
Cover Models Daria Rottenberk and Logan Parks

Manufactured in the United States of America

First Edition March 2018

ISBN-13: 978-1985796935 (Print edition only)
ISBN-10: 1985796937 (Print edition only)

For my wonderful little boy.
May your reality always be as extraordinary
as your imagination.

CHAPTER ONE

November

Sabrina

I threw back my shoulders and walked with purpose across the dark campus. It may have been three in the morning, *and* I may have been slightly buzzed, but I still made myself a promise. I was done being everyone's trusty sidekick. Trace freaking Forester, superstar wide receiver and one of the hottest guys I'd ever met, friend-zoned me, and I all but encouraged it.

What the hell was wrong with me?

"Hey," a deep voice called.

I stopped short, spinning to see if Forester changed his mind and followed me. He hadn't. That in itself sucked, but so did the knowledge that I was being followed in the middle of the effing night, alone on a huge campus with no mace or martial arts training. I doubted my flyer spot on my high school cheerleading squad would've done me any good now—two years later.

"Hey, blondie," the voice persisted.

I spun around, my now fading curls whipping around my head as I squinted into the darkness. The lights from the security phones cast a soft blue glow over the sidewalk, giving me the slightest sense of safety.

"Over here."

I spun again, this time noticing movement by a large tree. I focused, still struggling to discern who it was and wondering if I should run instead of stand there—like the victim in a horror movie giving the murderer time to catch her.

"You gonna stand there and stare or you gonna help me?" The annoyance in his voice—and the fact that he wasn't heavy breathing through a distorted mask—told me he wasn't a deranged slasher.

"Help you? I can't even see you."

"What the hell," he grumbled under his breath. "Come closer then."

I dug my hands into my hips. "Sorry if I'm reluctant to venture into the darkness because some stranger I can't see calls me over."

"Turn on your phone's light."

Huh. I hadn't thought of that.

I slipped my phone from the back pocket of my jeans and flashed my light on him. My eyes widened as I inhaled sharply. He definitely wasn't a masked murderer. He wasn't covered at all. He was butt-freaking-naked and tied to the trunk of a very large tree. The thick ropes binding him pinned his tattoo-covered arms to his sides.

"Why are you naked?" I asked.

"Naked? You wanna know why I'm naked?"

I nodded.

"So, the fact that I'm fucking bound to a tree is what? Not weird at all?"

I tried to keep my eyes on his, but the fact that my phone served as a wide spotlight on his naked body was a little distracting. "Sorry."

"Sorry?" His exasperation was palpable.

"Yeah. Sorry your nakedness surpassed the fact that you were kidnapped."

His face contorted. "Kidnapped? No one kidnapped me."

I lifted a knowing brow.

His face grew angry. "I get how it looks, but this ain't no kidnapping. It's an initiation…of sorts."

"You're pledging a frat?"

"Do I look like a frat boy to you?"

My eyes drifted over his naked body. His very impressive naked body. Whoever did this to him was kind enough to leave his goods on show for the world to see. And I wouldn't be a hot-blooded college girl if I didn't inspect his extraordinary package. "Hostile, cocky, and naked." My eyes lifted to his. "Total frat boy material."

"I need you to untie me," he ground out through clenched teeth.

"I didn't hear a please."

Given the deep growl in the back of his throat, it was becoming increasingly difficult for him to remain composed. "Could you *please* walk to the back of the tree and see if it's possible to untie the knots or if you need to go find a saw or something."

"A saw?"

He let out a long, frustrated breath.

"Just pointing out that a saw doesn't prove you're not some psycho murderer."

"What?"

"How do I know I'm not the one being set up? How do I know behind that tree isn't a group of guys ready to kidnap *me*?"

"I wasn't kidnapped," he growled.

"Says the guy tethered to a tree."

His head fell forward and he shook it. "If you're incapable of helping me, can you at least call someone who can?"

"I'm not incapable. Just skeptical."

"Jesus fucking Christ. The longer I'm trapped here, the closer to morning it gets. And while I know my body's breathtaking to women everywhere, I'd prefer not to have it plastered all over the Internet."

Breathtaking? Was this guy serious? I flashed my light around the area surrounding us. Nothing lurked. No strange sounds existed. He appeared to just be a guy caught in a very precarious situation. "Do you even go to this school?"

"Yes."

"Why haven't we met?"

"Because most nights I am not bound to a fucking tree," he snapped.

I walked closer to him, moving to the left and circling to the back of the tree. I stayed far enough away so if his ropes *were* an illusion and dropped from him if he stepped away from the tree, I could run. I flashed my phone around one last time, ensuring no one hid in the bushes before settling the beam on the knots holding him to the tree. Jesus Christ. "Did an entire Boy Scout troop do this to you?"

"Why? How many are there?"

"A lot." I switched off my light and tucked my phone into my pocket so I could use both hands. "Who'd you piss off?" I asked as I began picking away at the first knot on the top.

There was a long pause before he grumbled, "The hockey team."

"Did you hook up with one of their girlfriends or something?"

He shook his head. "I'm on the team."

"Your teammates did this to you?"

Another long pause. "I took the captain's position."

I pulled one of the ropes through a loop and untied the knot. "I got one. Twenty-something more to go."

"It'll be morning before you get them all done," he groaned. "Don't you have friends you can call?"

"They're all drunk at Forester's birthday."

"Should I know who that is?"

"Um, yeah. He's our school's star wide receiver. Probably going pro after this season. How don't you know that?"

"I don't follow football. And I just got here."

"It's November."

"I transferred."

"Mid-semester?"

"Anyone ever tell you that you ask a lot of questions?"

"Not every night I find a guy tied to a tree who tells me he transferred mid-semester."

"It's a long story."

"Not currently going anywhere."

He grumbled under his breath before relenting. "I didn't know I'd be taking the captain's position. You'd think they'd be kissing my fucking skates knowing I'm gonna win them a championship."

"Ever heard the saying there's no *I* in team?"

"Sweetheart, I am the team."

"Wow," I said, picking away at another one of the knots. "Conceited much?"

"Just speaking the truth."

"I wonder what they've got planned next." I hoped it was something good to teach this guy some humility.

He said nothing.

I somehow slipped a second knot free. "At least they gave you time to escape before the majority of campus woke up."

"Yeah. I'll be sure to thank them. What time is it?"

"Nearing four."

He huffed. "Think you could stop talking and work faster?"

Stop talking? Work faster? Who did he think he was? My fingers picked away at the next knot. It wasn't moving. No matter what I did, it was stuck. I moved to another. It was just as tight. I dug my fingernails in, but it was no use.

"Seriously? What's taking so damn long?" he grumbled as I fumbled away at the unwavering knots.

His tone and impatience with me caused my fingers to shake, rendering it impossible to untie another knot even if I wanted to.

"I'm talking to you," he said.

"Oh, I'm allowed to talk now?"

"Listen, I'm not looking to make friends. I need the damn knots untied."

I dropped the knot I'd been working on and rounded the tree. Stepping in front of him, I crossed my arms and met his angry eyes. "We, my friend, are at an impasse."

His eyes jumped between me and the ropes still holding him to the tree. "What the fuck?"

"I've been trying to help you. But it's four o'clock in the freaking morning. My fingertips are raw. And I'm doing the best I can. But what do I get?" I threw my arms into the air. "What do I always get? A whole lot of nothing. So, if you'll excuse me, this is my cue to exit. Good luck getting untied, but I'm starting to think you deserved it." I turned and walked away to the bellowing roar of the stranger yelling *bitch* into the darkness.

CHAPTER TWO

Sabrina

"You wanna grab lunch?" Finlay asked.

"Sure." I tossed down my phone and stood from my bed, smoothing out my white down comforter. "Where?"

"I told Caden we'd meet up with him at the dining hall. He's flying solo today. Forester apparently went home for his actual birthday."

I closed my eyes as the images from the previous night brought upon a body quaking cringe. Who pushes a totally hot guy toward another woman? *This girl.* I was hopeless. And in no condition to be told there were other fish in the sea. I saw what's in the sea, in the form of a guy tied to a tree, and if guys like that were the alternative, I'd rather be alone. "So, you expect me to be the third wheel again?"

"You know it's not like that."

"Says the one in love with Caden Brooks, superstar quarterback who only has eyes for her."

She groaned. "Would you stop? Caden likes having you around. He thinks you're hysterical."

"Oh, yeah. I'm just full of humor."

She tossed back her dark waves and laughed at my bleak tone. "I didn't tell him about your…experience last night."

"Why not? I thought you two share everything?"

"I wanted to hear you tell it again."

"So, I'm your entertainment today?"

She shrugged. "Something like that."

I grabbed my hoodie from the desk chair and walked to the door. "Fine. But I expect a captive audience."

"You got it."

* * *

"He said that?" Caden asked, wiping his mouth with a napkin.

I popped a small piece of a soft pretzel into my mouth. "Yup."

"While she was trying like hell to get him free," Finlay added, as if she'd been there.

"You guys see this?" a gruff voice asked.

I turned to find Grady, the football team's right tackle, sliding into the booth beside me. His big body pressed against me.

"What the hell, Grady?" Finlay snapped, beating me to it. Grady made her job as team water girl hell last year and she wouldn't let him forget it.

"See what?" Caden asked.

He held out his phone toward them.

Finlay's mouth dropped open before her eyes cut to mine. "You weren't lying." She grabbed Grady's phone and held it up for me to see. The picture filling the screen was a very naked hockey player tied to a tree. The only difference was he was there in broad daylight.

Caden glared at Grady. "Dude? You think I want you showing my girl pictures of some naked guy?"

"You feeling inadequate, Brooks?" Grady asked Caden.

"Is he still there?" I asked, stopping Caden from jumping across the table and beating the crap out of Grady.

Grady shook his head. "The fire department showed up to free him when I was doing the walk of shame."

"Serves him right," Finlay said.

Grady's eyes jumped between Caden and Finlay. "You know him?"

"Sabrina does," Caden said.

Grady looked to me. "Any idea what he did to piss someone off?"

I shrugged, not wanting to spread rumors about the hockey team. "How many people saw him?"

"Half the campus. People were posting pictures everywhere. You had to see the hordes of sorority girls showing up. Some were even posing with him." Grady grabbed a handful of Caden's fries and shoved them in his mouth. "The guy didn't stand a chance," he said with a mouthful. "He looked like he wanted to kill someone."

"How long did it take to get him free?" I asked.

"Don't know. The show ended as soon as they covered him up. Not too fun watching him get untied while covered up."

Finlay's brows shot up. "You prefer your guys naked, Grady?"

"Whoa. Retract the claws. I thought we had a truce?"

Her head recoiled. "Said who?"

Grady looked to Caden who shrugged.

"What the fuck?" Grady grumbled as he pushed his large body to his feet. "I'm outta here."

Once he was out of earshot, we all broke into laughter. Grady was one of the most unlikeable guys on campus. And even though he'd initially been an asshole to Finlay, we'd heard he wasn't the prick he wanted everyone to think he was. Finlay and I were still waiting for him to prove it, though.

"So, are you happy the dick got what he had coming?" Caden asked me.

"Yeah," I said, glancing out the window. The leaves on campus had begun to change color. Some had already fallen on the paths. Had Mr. Hockey noticed them as he stared out at the early morning campus before his world had been turned upside down even more?

* * *

I flew out the front door of my dorm and hurried toward my chem class. I picked up the pace as I trudged uphill, hoping like hell my professor hadn't sprung another surprise quiz on the class. I may not have been the most conscientious student—or declared a major yet for that matter, but I still cared about my grades and worked damn hard to make my parents proud. I was an only child which meant I needed my parents to see all their hard work raising me and carting me around to all my activities wasn't for naught. I wanted to be someone they were proud of.

Within minutes, I climbed the steps in front of the science building and rushed through the vacant foyer, taking the stairs two at a time. The sound of my Chucks echoed in the empty stairwell as I climbed the four flights to my classroom.

The squeaking of a door in the stairwell above, along with descending footsteps, stopped me in my tracks. I gasped, toppling back a few steps as Mr. Hockey nearly slammed into me as he rounded the corner, glaring like *I'd* done something wrong.

"Good to see you got yourself free," I said with as much snark as I could muster.

"No thanks to you."

"Seriously? You still can't see I was trying to help you? What's wrong with you?"

"Me? I didn't leave someone tied to a tree in the middle of the night."

"I think you're forgetting I tried to help you." I held up my calloused fingers. "Got the blisters to prove it."

"Right," he said doubtfully.

"Ever think the real reason they tied you to that tree wasn't because you took a stupid position, but because you're an asshole?"

His eyes narrowed.

The door in the stairwell above us slammed shut and footsteps bounded down the steps. The girl who was descending gave Mr. Hockey a salacious once-over. "Loved your pictures."

As if her attention erased the argument we'd been having, his entire face softened. His clouded eyes were now replaced by a vibrant blue. The angry creases around them eased, and the smile on his lips—a God damned *smile*—showed almost perfect teeth, aside from a tiny chip in his bottom front tooth. An obvious run-in with an angry puck. "Where you headed?" he asked the girl, his voice so smooth you could glide right over it.

"Back to my sorority house."

One of his dark brows arched. "Those the girls who came out to see me?"

She nodded.

"Then lead the way. I'd liked to meet them with my clothes on this time. Or…we could make it even and have them strip down."

She giggled, and everything about their exchange made my skin crawl. She moved by me, giving him just enough distance to check out her ass. And he did. Of course, he did.

Without another word, he glared at me, purposely bumping into me on his way down the stairs.

Their footsteps echoed in their wake as I stood alone in an empty stairwell hating Mr. Hockey more now than I had that night.

CHAPTER THREE

Sabrina

"Can you tell me why I'm here?" I asked from a chair in the dean's waiting room.

The dean's secretary, typing at her computer, didn't bother to look at me. "Dean Edwards will be with you shortly."

I pulled in an aggravated breath. I'd finished class and was heading back to the dorm. I needed an afternoon power nap like no one's business. But then her call came, requesting I stop in to speak with the dean as soon as I could. So, there I sat, wondering why the hell he wanted to see me.

The minutes crept by as I skimmed through the feed on my phone. As usual, lots was happening on campus. From sorority and fraternity fundraising events to fans in the football stadium, Alabama was a cool place to be. But I missed people like my best friend Trish back in my small Florida town. Thanks to social media I could catch up on what she'd been doing since we rarely had time to speak with our busy schedules. I skimmed through more pictures, memes, and ads. Naked pictures of an arrogant hockey player were no longer plastered in my newsfeed. Had the novelty worn off or had the people who'd posted them been ordered to take them down?

Dean Edwards' door opened. He stood with a kind smile in his charcoal three-piece suit looking at me like he already knew me, though I'd never spoken to him before. "Miss Marshall?"

I snatched up my bag and wrapped the strap across me as I stood, following him into his office.

He gestured to one of two leather chairs facing his oversized mahogany desk. "Have a seat." I did as he rounded his desk and sat across from me. "So, I'm sure you're wondering why I asked you here."

I nodded.

He leaned forward, folding his hands on the desk. "Well, as you know, we had quite the scene on campus this past weekend."

I tilted my head, knowing the time and place to use my blonde hair to my advantage. "I'm sorry?"

"The young man and the tree."

"Oh. Yeah. That was horrible."

"Any idea who did it?" he asked offhandedly, as if asking how I liked my coffee.

Was I going to implicate the entire hockey team for Mr. Hockey? For all I knew, he'd done more than he said and deserved it. "Do *you*?" I asked.

He shook his head. "That's why you're here, Miss Marshall. You were an eyewitness."

My stomach clenched, but I tried with everything I had to steel my features. "Said who?"

He swiveled the screen of his desktop monitor. A black and white surveillance video played. The view was a clear shot of the tree and a very naked Mr. Hockey. Oh, and me trying to untie him. *Shit.* "If you know I was there, why don't you know who did it?"

He turned the screen away from me. "The assailants wore masks."

"Well, if you don't know, how would I? I wasn't there when they tied him up. I just found him."

"You tried to help the young man. Surely, he said something."

I shook my head. "Did you ask him?"

"He's not talking."

My head snapped back. That didn't sound like Mr. Hockey. "I'm surprised he doesn't want whoever did it to be punished."

"Me too. Which leads me to believe they were people he knew." He sat back in his chair and crossed his arms. "Everyone knows I take campus hazing very seriously, Miss Marshall. This university comes down hard on anyone found partaking in it. So, I'm not letting this go. The guilty parties need to be punished."

I agreed completely. However, if Mr. Hockey didn't tell him, it wasn't my place to. He might've been an asshole, but for whatever reason, he didn't want the dean to know. "I'm sorry I can't help you, Dean Edwards."

His eyes assessed mine for a long uncomfortable moment. Could he tell I was hiding something? Could he see Mr. Hockey told me who did it? Was he waiting me out? He blinked a few times before standing from his desk. "Well, thanks for stopping by."

I jumped to my feet, elated to be dismissed.

"Please let me know if you remember anything. Even if you think it's minor, it could help."

I nodded as I turned to walk away.

"Oh, and Miss Marshall?"

I spun back around.

"Do you make a habit of leaving people tied to trees in the middle of the night?"

My body tensed. "Excuse me?"

"I just can't figure why you didn't call for help."

What was he implying? Did he think I had something to do with it? Did he think I was a horrible person? Was I? "I'll let you know if I remember anything." I turned on shaky legs and made my way out of his office before he could say another word.

I stepped outside into the cool November day wondering if I'd done the right thing. Students rushed by me, hurrying to their next classes as the dean's words rattled around in my head. I may not have been studying to be a brain surgeon, but I knew a threat when I heard one.

* * *

I walked up the sidewalk of a house on the outskirts of campus, cursing every slow step I took and wondering if I should turn back around.

"Hot damn," a deep voice called from the open front door.

I stared into the eyes of Grady, hating that I'd been forced to be there. "Is anyone else home?" I purposely looked behind him, hoping someone would be around to protect me from the big oaf.

A smile slid across his face. "Nope. Just you and me, babe. I knew it was only a matter of time before you came begging me for it."

My entire face scrunched in disgust. "Hell has definitely not frozen over yet."

Grady's footsteps resounded down the front steps until he stood towering in front of me. "Why you such a hater, girl?"

I stared up at him. He was a huge guy, but his face had slimmed down since last year. I hadn't noticed at lunch when he was shoving Mr. Hockey's naked body in my face. "I didn't come here to be hit on."

"Do you know how many girls would love to be on the receiving end of my attention?"

I pretended to think about it, using my fingertips as a calculator. "None?"

His head dropped back on a groan. "You're impossible."

"You're single-minded."

"Have you looked in a mirror? You're gorgeous. You can't blame a guy for trying."

I cocked my head, staring at his pathetic attempt at a goatee. Could I ignore all his lame advances in order to get his help? Could I see the good in Grady that Caden tried to assure us lingered underneath the surface?

"Come on," he backed down. "You must really need something if you came here to see me."

"I do."

He swept out his arm toward the two-story house behind him. "Lead the way. Just ignore the smell. I live with four other dudes. You know how it is."

"Let's sit on the steps. This won't take long."

"Said who?"

I brushed by him and headed toward the front steps. "You can't help yourself, can you?"

"It's a gift."

I shook my head, stifling my unwarranted amusement as I sat down on the top step.

He sat down beside me, the side of his big body pressing against mine. "Now, what can I do for you?"

"I heard you're studying pre-law."

"I am. Are you into smart guys?"

"I'm into guys who can have an entire conversation without hitting on me."

"I make no promises."

I rolled my eyes.

"Okay, fine. Why do you wanna know what I'm studying? You having some legal troubles?"

I drew in a deep breath as I chose my words wisely. "The dean thinks I know something, and I think he just threatened me because of it."

His head shot back. "That's a pretty big accusation. Are you sure?"

I shook my head. "No. That's why I'm here."

"So, let me ask you something. Do you know what he thinks you know?"

I nodded. "But it didn't come from a reliable source."

"Then why not tell him that?"

"Because if I do, it could get quite a few people in trouble, and possibly expelled."

He nodded his understanding.

"I need to know what my rights are."

"Babe, I'm not even in law school yet. I only know pretty basic laws. But my uncle's got a law firm in Montgomery. Would you mind if I checked with him?"

"No, that would be awesome."

He pulled his phone from his pocket and handed it to me. "Let me get your number. I'll call you tonight when I hear back from him. He's in the courtroom all day."

I leveled him with serious eyes as I took his phone. "If I start getting pictures of your package, I *will* come and kill you."

He smirked. "Don't be so sure. I've been told it's one of Alabama's most prized landmarks."

"You're sick, you know that, right?" I said, placing a quick call to my phone from his so he had my number.

"It's another gift."

This time I laughed. The guy wasn't half bad, as long as he kept his mouth shut.

CHAPTER FOUR

Crosby

"What the hell does that mean?" I growled into the phone as I stood in the empty hallway outside the locker room in nothing but a towel.

"It means your parents' assets will remain frozen until they're disseminated to those they stole from," their lawyer explained. "This is just the beginning of a long legal process."

"I get that, but what about me? What about my trust funds? There has to be something available."

"Crosby. You're at Alabama because there are no more trust funds. I thought you understood that? Seems the dean and your coach are the few people your parents didn't steal from. They did you a real solid by getting you in there."

I could feel my anger pulsating through my body. My muscles tensed and my heartbeat pounded in my temples. "Despite what you think, I'm not some dumb jock. I do understand what's happening. I just don't understand why I can't have the money in my name."

"Because your parents were the account custodians. The money isn't actually yours."

I dropped my head against the concrete wall behind me.

"Remember why you're in Alabama, Crosby. Fly under the radar and make it to the pros. Then no one can touch the money you make."

I disconnected the call feeling worse than I had before.

No one had been straight with me. Everyone had been feeding me bullshit since my parents were sent to prison. 'Don't worry, Crosby, we'll appeal the ruling.' 'Don't worry, Crosby, you have your trust funds.' 'Don't worry, Crosby. We'll keep your mom out of it.' 'Don't worry, Crosby, you'll be okay.' And since then, I haven't been okay. Not even close. My parents didn't have a chance in hell of winning their appeal. And my trust funds weren't fucking mine. My entire life had been turned upside down and there wasn't a damn thing I could do about it. Not a damn thing but play hockey and go to school as if I was actually going to be okay someday.

But the truth was I had no one. Everyone who'd been in my life when the money was there quickly disappeared when it was gone. That or they'd been the same people my father embezzled from.

My father was a mean son of a bitch who was the sole heir to my grandfather's investment company. When my grandfather died, it was just my father running things. The only reason people came around him was because of his money. No one could've imagined the greedy bastard was making himself richer by skimming off other people's investment earnings. With no money, he was a broke son-of-a-bitch who brought his wife down with him.

Now they were spending the rest of their lives in jail.

I'd thought about it relentlessly. About the signs. About their hushed conversations. And still, I couldn't be sure he'd always been crooked. All I knew was we'd been rich. I never questioned it. At sixteen, I had my own

Lamborghini. You don't question a damn thing when life is that good. You question everything once it goes south. And you realize your wealth was due to everyone else's loss.

Sabrina

I rounded the corner in the hockey arena, on a mission to find Mr. Hockey. My footsteps faltered when I found him standing outside the locker room in nothing but a towel hanging low on his hips. His eyes were closed and his head rested against the wall behind him. His cell phone was clutched in his hand at his side.

Seeing him in darkness was one thing. But seeing him in broad freaking daylight was something else entirely. The vibrancy of the colorful sleeves of tattoos wrapped around his arms were a stark contrast to his ink-free chest. The same bare chest, with chiseled abs, that left little to the imagination yet so much to be desired. And as much as I hated to admit it, knowing what hung under that towel did a number on my determined mind.

I shook my head, clearing away the unwelcome thoughts. "Why didn't you rat them out?"

His head flew off the wall, visibly startled by my presence. "What?"

I lifted my chin toward the locker room doorway as I passed by it before stopping in front of him. "Why didn't you rat them out?"

His face scrunched in confusion. "How do you know I didn't?"

"Well, for one, I got called into the dean's office."

"Why?"

"He has video footage from—"

He stepped off the wall and grabbed my arm so quickly, I had no time to resist. He pulled me away from the locker room and stopped us in the corner, practically caging me in.

"That night," I finished, wrenching my arm free from his grip. "It looked like it came from a nearby building."

"I know."

"You know? Then why didn't you let their asses fry?"

His eyes jumped around, his mouth opening then closing just as quickly.

"Dean Edwards all but threatened me to come up with something," I continued. "He thinks I know who did it."

"You do."

"So do you."

He crossed his arms. And I hated that, as angry as I was, I couldn't stop from noticing the way his biceps bulged.

Focus, Sabrina. Focus.

"I'm not about to pretend this makes sense. But if this touches me, I have no problem telling him what I know." I spun away from him and took off down the hallway.

"But you didn't," he called.

I stopped and glanced over my shoulder at him standing there in his towel. "Because *you* didn't. I assumed there was a reason."

His lips twisted as he seemed to ponder my words.

I didn't wait for his response. If I had, I had a feeling I would have been waiting for a long freaking time. I turned and left him standing alone in that empty hallway.

CHAPTER FIVE

Sabrina

You know that feeling you get when you sense someone staring at you? Well that's the feeling I got as soon as I sat down in my communications class the following day. My eyes cut to the right and sure enough Jeremy, the tall guy beside me, stared at me.

"You have a minute to talk after class?" he asked.

I nodded, knowing we only ever spoke about upcoming tests or assignments. I hoped like hell he wasn't looking for a tutor.

After class I tucked my book and laptop into my messenger bag, wondering if he planned to speak to me there or outside the building.

"So," he said once the other students exited the classroom.

"So."

"I wanted to talk to you."

"Yup. I got that when you said you wanted to talk to me after class."

He laughed, and it was a damn sexy laugh. It complemented his tall, dark, and athletic build. "Keep them on their toes my grandmother always told me," he said.

He had a sexy laugh *and* he was quoting his freaking granny. This was getting interesting.

He stood from his seat and leaned back against his desk. "I was wondering if you're seeing anyone."

I grabbed my bag and stood. "Not currently."

His smile broadened. "Could I take you out tomorrow night?"

Straightforward and no games. I liked that in a guy. "Tomorrow night?"

"Unless you're busy."

"I'm not busy."

He smiled. "Does seven work?"

"Sure."

He pulled out his phone and handed it to me. "Let me get your number in case my practice runs late."

I punched my number into his contacts. "What do you play?"

"Oh, I thought you knew. Hockey."

A humorless laugh shot out of me. What was it with me and hockey players? I'd been surrounded by football players since last year when Finlay started dating Caden, now suddenly the hockey players were coming out of the woodwork. The universe was definitely toying with me.

I handed him back his phone. "I'm in Carver Hall. Text and I'll come down."

He nodded. "Great. See you later, Sabrina."

I watched him walk out of the classroom wondering why I'd never paid him much attention before. *Had* I been hoping Trace Forester would come around? Had I been closed off to other possibilities? Had I been too wrapped up in everyone else's lives to focus on my own?

* * *

I stared into the mirror in the girls' restroom. I'd applied minimal makeup, opting for only smoky eyes for my date with Jeremy, unsure where we were even going. My phone vibrated on the sink. I hit speaker while touching up the corners of my eyes. "Hello?"

"What are you wearing?" Grady asked. "Please tell my lingerie."

"Do I need to hang up?"

"This hard-to-get thing is gettin' old."

A toilet flushed in a stall behind me. A girl who lived down the hall stepped out stifling a smile.

"Yeah. I totally want you," I said to Grady as I rolled my eyes at the girl stepping up beside me to wash her hands. "I just like the chase. And I want you to keep using lame lines on me. It's totally hot."

"Whoa. Easy," he said. "They're not lame. Lines like mine take weeks to perfect."

The girl laughed as she dried her hands and walked toward the door. "Good luck with that one."

"Is there someone else there?" Grady asked. "You having one of those sexy pillow-fight slumber parties? I'd be happy to stop by and provide entertainment."

"Why is it that guys think we actually have pillow fights?"

"It's the visual, babe. It carries us through those lonely nights."

"So, every night for you?"

"Pretty much," he agreed.

I snickered. "So, is there a reason for this call or are you just trying to torture me?"

"I talked to my uncle," he said, his voice becoming serious.

I switched the phone off speaker and lifted it to my ear. "Okay."

"Knowing what he knows about Dean Edwards, he said he thinks the dean's less likely to be threatening you and more likely to be trying to come down hard on hazing."

"That's what he said in his office."

"Well, apparently, he's up for re-election and doesn't want any bad press getting in the way."

"So, does this mean you know why he called me in?" I said.

"Everybody knows."

"Great," I mumbled.

"My uncle said he doubts he'll call you back in, but if he does, call me and I'll let my uncle know. He said do *not* speak to him without someone there with you."

"Okay."

"Don't worry," Grady said. "He thinks the dean's covering his own ass. He's as eager to eliminate damaging publicity from the school as you are to stay out of it."

As much as I wanted to believe that, I couldn't forget the disgust in the dean's words or the look in his eyes when he called me out for leaving Mr. Hockey alone out there.

On the way back to my room, I received a text from Jeremy. "His practice ran long," I announced to Finlay as I stepped back into our room. "He wants me to meet him at the rink."

"Hey, at least he called," Finlay said, her laptop in front of her as she sprawled out on the floor typing a paper. "The guys on the football team have to run laps if they're caught with their phones anywhere near the field. He must've snuck away to contact you."

I walked over to the mirror and checked my face again. "Yeah, I guess."

"Hey."

I glanced at her through the mirror.

"Don't sabotage this before it even begins," she said, sounding like a concerned mama bear.

"Sabotage would indicate premeditation."

She tilted her head. "For the past year and a half, I've watched you blow off guys who were interested while you gave your attention to the ones who weren't available." She coughed. "Trace Forester."

I turned from the mirror and glared at her. "I never had a thing for Forester."

She rolled her eyes. "*Riiiiight.*"

"Fine. I agree he's hot. But totally corny."

"Don't tell him that."

"Too late."

Her shoulders shook with laughter.

"Well, no need to worry." I grabbed my fitted leather jacket from the closet and walked to the door. "I plan on giving Jeremy a chance. Now how do I look?"

Finlay's eyes drifted over my skinny jeans and the low-cut black top I paired with a chunky turquoise necklace. "Hot."

"Obviously." I laughed before turning and heading out.

I arrived at the rink after a short walk and tugged on the front door. It was locked. I glanced around. If not for the cars in the dimly lit parking lot, I would've thought I'd been set up. The campus was quiet. No one walked around. That was the crazy thing about a huge campus. It could change from chaotic during the day to deserted at night. I preferred the solace to the chaos any day.

The creaking of the arena door behind me had me spinning around.

An older man stood with the door cracked open. "Can I help ya?"

"I'm meeting one of the players here."

"The boys are still on the ice. Coach is running their butts into it tonight." He waved me inside. "No use waiting out there. Come take a seat inside."

Inside, whistles echoed and blades scraped the ice. Heavily padded guys raced across the slick surface. I took a seat in the front corner of the arena, trying to remain out of sight. The man hadn't said it was a closed practice, but the locked door indicated otherwise.

"Faster," the coach bellowed from the center of the ice as the players skated in what looked like suicides from one side of the rink to the other.

I searched for Jeremy but had no clue what number he wore. Hockey wasn't a sport I followed. It seemed exciting, but when you went to school in Alabama, you cheered on the football team.

When the whistle blew again, the guys skated over to the bench and grabbed their water bottles. A few pulled off their helmets. Their cheeks were red and their sweat-drenched hair hung in their faces. Hockey was clearly more intense than I gave it credit for. My eyes snagged on the inky black hair of my nemesis. His eyes were pinned on mine.

I lifted my hand, as if to wave at him, but turned it instead, bending all but my middle finger.

Mr. Hockey laughed. The bastard laughed.

The coach blew his whistle again, and the guys skated back out onto the ice.

Crosby

"*Oouff.*" I shook off yet another hit and skated after the puck in our end-of-practice scrimmage. I was determined like hell to show the amateurs on the team, and the Ice Queen who sat in the seats, what a real hockey player looked like. Forget my opponents, if I was gonna get the shit beat out of me on the ice by my own teammates, I was gonna make damn sure they looked like they weren't fit to clean my skates.

I'd been the top scorer on my team in Texas for the past three years. Pro scouts had been talking to my coaches. *And*, I'd just been named captain.

Then shit hit the fan and I ended up in Alabama.

Now my teammates back home—my *brothers*—wanted nothing to do with me, feeling like I abandoned them when we had a shot at the championship. I didn't blame them for feeling that way, but I did blame them for deserting me and not having my back when I needed friends more than ever. Of course, some of them had reason to want nothing to do with me. My father had chummed it up with their parents, persuading them to invest with him. We all know how that turned out.

Somehow my new teammates caught wind of my successes on the ice. They also knew I already had one foot out the door, planning to enter the pro draft after this season. And they hated me for it.

I couldn't help that I was skilled. I should've gone pro this year, but I'd promised my mom, after everything she'd been through, that I'd graduate before entering the draft. And since that's all she had to hang on to, I needed to stay true to my words.

But I had news for my new teammates. Their jealousy and quest to make my transition to the team difficult were not standing in the way of me getting drafted. I would take what they dished and stay the fuck off the dean's radar.

All I needed to do was graduate. Then I could leave Alabama and everyone in it behind.

"I like what I've been seeing out there," Coach said as we formed a circle around him at the end of practice. "I have no idea where this newfound intensity's coming from, but I like it."

Half the team's eyes suddenly avoided Coach's. I should've turned around and shown him the big bullseye on my back.

"Just remember," Coach continued. "You guys are on the same team. You can practice with intensity, but I don't want anyone hurt, especially before next week's game. Go hit the showers." He looked to me. "Crosby. I wanna speak with you."

The others filed off the ice. More than one shot me a glare.

Assholes.

Once Coach and I were alone, he pegged me with his eyes. "Anything you wanna tell me?"

"Nope."

"So, you're fine with your teammates resenting your skills?"

"Didn't realize they felt that way."

He cocked his head, not buying the blatant lie. Even though I hadn't ratted out the team for the tree stunt, everyone—even Coach—assumed it had been my teammates. "I know things have been tough for you. And if you're feeling like they're not treating you like one of their own, you need to let me know."

"I'm twenty-one. Not five."

He nodded. "I get that. But I don't want anything outside the game affecting you. You've stayed consistent on the ice despite everything that happened in Texas. I don't want guys, who aren't playing this game as a potential career, hurting your chances at the pros."

I shrugged, though I doubted he could tell with my pads on.

"I'm serious, Crosby. Make it through this season playing like you have been, and the draft is within your grasp."

Sabrina

I checked my watch. Jeremy knew I was there, gesturing to me to wait as he hurried into the locker room.

I watched as Mr. Hockey spoke to the coach. Was he being reprimanded for having a poor attitude or something else? Because the post-practice lecture couldn't be about his skills on the ice. Given his fluid movements out there and the ease in which he handled a stick, the guy could seriously play—despite the hard hits he took from his teammates.

The coach stepped away from him and gathered some things from the bench. Mr. Hockey's eyes found mine once again, and he skated toward me.

I swallowed down my surprise as I stood, pretending not to notice him skating my way.

His body was big, but he moved with such grace and agility, as if skating was as normal as walking for him. He pushed open the door of the rink wall. "You stalking me now?"

I crossed my arms and cocked my head, wishing the idiot would've forgotten we'd ever met. "I'm not here for you."

Even with his helmet on I could see his arched brow. "Oh no?"

I stood tight-lipped. I didn't owe him anything.

"Don't tell me you're dating one of these guys."

"Maybe I am."

His face sobered and, strangely, anger brimmed in his eyes. "Who?"

"None of your business."

His head jolted back. "You don't think I can find out?"

"I don't care if you do. I'm just not telling you."

"What, are you in first grade?"

I glared into his eyes, hoping he could see the hatred I felt toward him.

"Well, enjoy yourself with the mystery prick."

"Who said he's a prick?"

"They all are." He turned and skated back down the ice, nabbing a puck from the side with his stick. He skated around the perimeter of the rink, moving the puck around before firing it at the net.

I checked my phone. It was already seven-thirty. I wondered where Jeremy and I would go. I knew nothing about him, so I had no idea what he had planned. Dinner. A movie.

"So, let me guess, you're banging Potter."

I glanced up. Mr. Hockey stood in front of me again, his dark hair falling into his eyes now that he'd removed his helmet and held it in his hand. "I'm not banging anyone."

"But that's who you're going out with, isn't it?"

"Maybe."

His eyes narrowed. "When did he ask you out?"

"Why does that matter?"

"It just does."

"Yesterday. Happy?"

"You always make yourself available that easily?"

My teeth ground together. "I don't like your implication."

He shrugged. "The guy's a prick."

"Takes one to know one."

He chuckled, and the sound pissed me off more than if he had called me a bitch again. "So, the ice queen has a sense of humor."

My eyes widened as my arms dropped down to my sides. "Ice queen? Ever think it's you? Ever think that maybe every word out of your mouth makes my skin crawl?"

His lips slipped into a cocky grin. "So, you're saying I affect you?"

I growled as my hands bunched into fists. This guy had serious split personality issues. Even still, no one made me as angry—or as capable of growling—as him. "Apparently, you only hear what you want to hear. Do you take meds for that?"

A sober laugh slipped from his lips. "Have fun with your date. I wouldn't let him get in your panties if you know what I mean."

"Of course I don't know what you mean. I don't speak idiot."

He stifled a smile. "Just saying I saw the prescription cream he's got in his bag. Wouldn't want you catching anything."

"Well, that's where you and I are different. I'd love for *you* to catch something."

He tsked. "Careful. I might mistake this anger for sexual tension."

I scoffed. "You're insane."

"I'm not the one going out with a prick."

I huffed, his annoying taunts working my last nerve.

"You ever wonder why he asked you out?" he asked.

"What?"

"Why, out of all the girls on campus, he asked *you* out?"

"Because I'm amazing?"

He snickered, and I suddenly wanted to punch him in the face and chip his other tooth. "Interesting timing don't you think?"

"We sit next to each other in Communications."

"Exactly. Why hasn't he asked you out before now?"

"Do you make a habit of losing people because you seriously make no sense to me at all."

"Hey," Jeremy called.

Mr. Hockey and I both turned.

Jeremy stood on the platform to my right all showered and dressed. I hadn't even heard him approach. "You okay?"

I crossed my arms as if I needed them to protect me from the craziness around me. "Fine."

"Yes. She. Is." Mr. Hockey said, annunciating each word as his eyes drifted up my body.

Jeremy and I both glared at him.

He remained unfazed. "Have fun tonight you crazy kids. Remember what I said, Ice Queen."

Jeremy looked to me as Mr. Hockey skated away in no particular hurry. "You know him?"

"Not really."

"Well, take it from me, the guy's a total douche."

I laughed, and the tension from my exchange with Mr. Hockey lifted slightly by the assurance in Jeremy's words.

* * *

I twirled my spaghetti around my fork as I listened to Jeremy speak about growing up in Alabama. Our conversation flowed so easily. I felt myself drawn in by his adorable southern accent, the slow drawl making me hang on every syllable.

"So, what made a boy from Alabama play hockey?"

"Are you kidding? The fights."

I laughed before taking a bite of my pasta.

He sipped his tall glass of beer, having already finished his meal. "How about you? You play any sports?"

I shook my head. "I may be a total daddy's girl, but he never could get me to play anything for more than a season. I cheered. That's where I gained my love for football. That and the hot guys."

He laughed. "We hockey players aren't so bad."

I nodded. "I'm starting to see that."

He looked away, almost sheepishly, and I liked knowing I affected him.

"So, what's the deal with Mr. Hockey?" I asked.

His eyes shot back to mine. "Mr. Hockey?"

"Yeah. Douchebag who got himself tied to a tree."

Laughter burst out of him. "You call him Mr. Hockey?"

I shrugged. "I don't know his name."

"You don't know who he is?"

I lifted my glass to my lips and sipped my water. "I just said that."

"His name's Crosby. Something happened at his last school that got him shipped here."

I placed down my glass curious about what Crosby had done to get himself shipped off to Alabama mid-semester. Had he slept with the dean's daughter? Hazed a freshman? Fought his coach? He'd told me he transferred, but after that night, I hadn't given it another thought. "What happened?"

Jeremy shrugged, but something flashed across his eyes that told me he knew more than he was saying.

"I heard he stole your captain's position."

"He didn't steal my position," Jeremy said, a sudden coolness in his voice.

Whoops. "I didn't know you were the captain."

"I *am* the captain. No one's taking that from me."

Whoa boy. "That's not why you guys tied him to a tree?"

His brows pinched in the middle. "Who said we tied him to a tree?"

I looked for a shred of guilt—or coyness for that matter—behind his eyes. But either he was a great actor *or* he really had nothing to do with it because I found nothing. "I just got the feeling it was some type of initiation thing."

"The guy's a jackass. Don't feel sorry for him."

I grabbed a slice of Italian bread and tore a small piece from it. "For what it's worth, he seems to hate being here as much as you hate having him on your team." I popped the piece of bread into my mouth.

He scoffed.

"And whether or not you did tie him up, those knots were freaking tight."

Jeremy laughed. "Oh, that's right. I think I heard you were the one who found him."

"Lucky me."

"He didn't say who did it?" he asked, his eyes hyper-focused on mine.

I took my last bite of pasta before shaking my head.

"I hear the dean's looking to punish whoever did it," he said.

I shrugged. If I didn't rat out the hockey team to the dean, I wasn't about to say anything to Jeremy. What good would it do? He clearly had something to do with it. He wouldn't have been so eager to hear my side if he hadn't.

"Did the dean call you in?" he persisted.

"Yeah."

"Geez." I could see in his jumpy eyes that he wasn't finished with his questions. "So, what'd you tell him?"

I lifted one shoulder, hoping he took the hint I didn't like being interrogated. "Nothing."

"Nothing?"

"I know nothing, so I told him nothing."

His face softened, as if a weight had lifted off his shoulders. "That's good."

I lifted my chin at his black leather wristband, changing the subject as quickly as I could. "I like that."

He lifted his wrist to give me a better view. "My mom gave it to me after I scored the game-winning goal last year."

"What's on it?" I asked, inspecting its small silver plate.

"She had it engraved. 'Potters Never Give Up.'"

"Were you thinking of quitting hockey?"

He shook his head. "Just an inside thing, I guess."

I smiled. "So, you guys gonna win this year, or what?"

Jeremy smiled, and just like that, our night was salvaged and Crosby's name never came up again.

Crosby

My hands pressed into the shower tiles in front of me. The spray rained over my head and the back of my neck, releasing all the tension in my body. Practice had been a killer. It sucked having to be civil with the pricks on my team, especially since I didn't know who tied me up. I closed my eyes as the water continued washing over me. Images from that night flooded my brain.

The air was so fucking cold on my bare skin, but I wouldn't let them see it affected me. I held my chin in the air and took it like the man I was. After, of course, I'd fought like an animal to resist the ropes. But four on one wasn't easy, no matter how strong I was. Figuring it was part of my initiation to the hockey team, I relented, hoping they were just trying to scare me and would eventually release me.

I'd only been on campus a day, so I knew no one. And because the cowards wore masks, I could only hear their voices and the orders barked out by their leader. I tried to commit them to memory so I could put the voices with faces once I began practicing with the team. But when you're naked, cold, and fucking pissed, it's easier said than done.

"Tie the knots tighter," the leader barked again, as the three others worked from behind the tree. If this was all a big show, they were spending a whole lot of time securing me in place.

Their leader, who was about my height and build, paced in front of me, directing none of his comments to me.

"What do you get out of this?" I asked him.

He turned slowly. Beneath his dark mask, I could see his beady narrow eyes, but still he said nothing to me.

"I get the whole haze the rookie thing, but I'm gonna be one of your best players. I'm gonna help the team win. Why do this? Why humiliate me?"

One of the guys behind me laughed. "He's never gettin' out of these."

One of the other guys said, "Yeah, he'll probably still be here when classes start on Monday."

I tried to move my arms, but they'd pulled the ropes so damned tight they were cutting into my skin. And to make matters worse, they were right. I was stuck there until someone showed up on Monday. A day and a half away.

The guys stepped out from behind me and walked over to their leader. "Dude, he's not going anywhere," one of them said.

"Head back," the leader said. "I'll meet you there."

Like meek children, the three of them turned and did as told. Were they scared of this guy?

Once they disappeared into the darkness, he stopped pacing and stepped right up to me. "We know you're using our team as a stepping stone for your career," he said, low and menacing. "But let me make something very clear. We don't like being used, and we don't plan on making your time here easy."

"I can take whatever you've got."

"Damn straight you will. Or, I assure you, you'll never see the pros."

I opened my eyes, pushing away the anger I felt every time I remembered that night. Every time I remembered why I needed to put up with their shit. Every time I heard my parents' lawyer telling me not to blow the chance I had at a bright future—one that didn't involve my parents or what they'd done to tarnish all of our names. Every time I wanted to kick the shit out of every last one of these guys.

CHAPTER SIX

Sabrina

"He was nice."

"Just nice?" Finlay asked, chewing down her cheeseburger in the dining hall.

"Okay fine. He was a freaking beast. The guy could go all night long."

Finlay's eyes widened. "Liar."

"Hey, if you didn't stay at Caden's last night, you would've been there when he had his way with me on your bed."

"Shut up," she said.

"You'll never know."

"I already know," she said. "I can see it all over your face. It's not there. If it was, you'd have those big blue gaga eyes you get."

My nose wrinkled. "Gaga eyes?"

She nodded. "All dreamy and captivated. The way you get around Forester. You play indifferent, but I know the truth."

"You do, huh?"

She nodded.

I rolled my eyes. "I'm done being into guys who are into someone else. I want someone who wants me as much as I want him. I deserve that."

"You do deserve that. You need someone who makes you feel larger than life."

"And gives me gaga eyes."

She laughed before mowing down the rest of her burger. The girl could seriously eat anything and not gain a pound. I, on the other hand, had to watch everything I ate. I wasn't very tall, so the curves I had were a minute away from becoming rolls if I wasn't careful. "I think I know what your problem is."

"Oh, yeah?" I asked curiously.

"You think love should be difficult."

I scoffed. "Not true. My parents never fight and they're happy—"

"And boring," Finlay said, holding up her palms. "Your words not mine."

Was she right? Did I think love should be more of a challenge?

"How'd your date go?" a deep voice asked.

My head flew to my left.

Crosby slipped into the seat beside me.

"What are you doing?"

"Asking how your date went."

I eyed the scarce space he'd left between us. "No, I mean, why are you sitting here?"

He glanced to Finlay. "Is she a little slow?"

Finlay shook her head, her eyes assessing him. She'd only heard stories about my unwanted run-ins with the infamous Crosby, so I wondered what ran through her mind.

"Why do you care how my date went?" I asked him.

"Just curious if you let him get into your panties."

My eyes flared. I glanced to Finlay who stared across the table, her eyes jumping between the two of us.

"Who are you?" she asked, both amused and confused.

He reached his hand across the table toward her. "Crosby. I figured your girl told you all about me."

She stared at his hand still hovering in the air and made no attempt to shake it. "Afraid not," she lied, like the true friend she was.

"That's surprising. We shared some memorable moments together." He lowered his hand and glanced back to me. "Well? Was I right about his condition?"

"Why are you so interested in my sex life? You're never gonna be part of it."

"Never say never."

I glanced to Finlay who tried unsuccessfully to stifle a smile. "What are you smiling about?"

"You two are funny."

"Funny?" I asked, my exasperation peaking.

She nodded. "And he's hotter than in the picture."

My mouth dropped open. What the hell was she trying to do?

"She's been looking at pictures of me?" he asked Finlay as he swept his hand through his dark hair, definitely working the fact she called him hot.

"Everyone's seen pictures of you," I snapped. "Tied to a tree. Remember?"

He raised a brow at my suddenly traitorous friend. "She's been trolling me on social media, hasn't she?"

"You're so annoying," I growled, wanting nothing more than to storm out of there like a spoiled child.

"Ladies seem to like me fine the way I am."

"I bet you get gaga eyes from them," Finlay added, clearly for my benefit.

He tilted his head to the side. "I get a *lot* of things from them."

I grabbed my bag and stood. "And the hockey team."

"Low blow," he said, feigning hurt. "Even for you, Ice Queen."

"It's been great catching up, but I'm outta here." I spun away from them and stormed off.

"She always that difficult?" he asked Finlay as I moved away from them.

"When she hates someone? Yes."

Crosby

I walked into the locker room after our first win. Most of the guys had already showered and were in different stages of dress while I opted for more ice time to work on my shot. I may have scored two of the four goals, but I wasn't satisfied with my form.

No one acknowledged me as I walked to my locker, removed my gloves and helmet, and stuffed them into my bag. It was weird. I was getting used to the silence that surrounded me. Used to the fact that this was like some crazy fraternity that didn't want me. But the joke was on them. They were a means to an end for me. Nothing else.

I removed more of my gear, pulling off my shoulder pads and wincing at the pain emanating from my shoulder. As much as I wanted to slather on some pain-relieving gel, I wouldn't let them see they'd hurt me. Fuck 'em.

I grabbed a towel from the pile by my locker and stripped off the rest of my clothes, stuffing them into the laundry pile the equipment manager took care of for us. I wrapped the towel around my waist and walked into the showers. Inside the stall, the warm water cascaded over my body. The sound of the droplets raining down and forming puddles at my feet soothed me, drowning out the noise in my head. I stood there for a long time letting the heat of the water ease the pain in my achy muscles. I'd still need to alternate between ice and heat when I got back to the dorm, though. I usually had to do that on game nights, but now practices were just as brutal.

One thing I did feel good about was my run-in with the ice queen. She appeared unscathed after her date with Jeremy. It wasn't like I could come right out and tell her she was being used. Maybe they'd make a happy couple. Who the fuck knew…

Once the water turned cold and my balls were pruned to the size of walnuts, I switched off the shower and reached for my towel from the hook outside the stall. It wasn't there. I stuck my head out and looked down on the tile floor hoping it had fallen. It hadn't.

Fuck.

I stepped out of the shower and walked into the now deserted locker room. The pile of towels I sought had disappeared and so had everything in my locker. Everything but my skates and jockstrap.

God dammit.

I closed my eyes and held back my anger. At least I tried to, but I was seeing a whole lot of red behind my closed eyelids. I dragged in a long breath before opening my eyes and scanning the lockers around me. None of them had anything in them but bottles of shampoo, deodorant, and razors. Nothing I could use to cover up.

Sons of bitches.

I covered my dick and glanced toward Coach's office. He wanted to know how the guys had been treating me. Wanted to know if I felt like part of the team. As much as I wanted to rat them out *and* ask for something to wear home, I knew it would be stirring up shit I didn't need.

So, I did the only thing I could. I grabbed the jockstrap from my locker and slipped it on, making my way out of the arena. It would take a lot more than some lame hazing to get me to quit the team.

The sun had set hours before, but students still walked around. If the entire campus hadn't already seen my goods, I may have been more embarrassed. Still, I wished I had a car—if only mine hadn't been repossessed. At least I still had what the good Lord gave me. Two feet. Two very bare feet that would carry me across campus and back to my dorm in a fucking jockstrap.

The looks, catcalls, and cars honking would've been enough to make a weaker man crumble. But I'd been through hell. This was child's play.

As I moved closer to the dorms, a horn honked beside me and I flipped the driver the bird.

"That the way you want to treat your savior?" a girl asked.

I peeked over.

The ice queen's friend sat in the driver's seat of an old pickup truck that had pulled up to the curb beside me. "Get in."

I didn't even think about it. I walked right to the passenger door and pulled it open. The vinyl bench seat gave me pause, knowing my ass cheeks would stick to it.

She laughed, reaching behind the seat and grabbing a blanket. She handed it to me.

"Thanks." I took it and wrapped it around my waist before climbing inside the truck.

She shifted the truck into gear and pulled away from the sidewalk. "You know I'm gonna have to ask."

"It was a joke."

"I work for the football team." Her eyes jumped between me and the campus road. "Guys can be tough on the rookies. It'll get better. Just don't be an ass and provoke them."

"I see why you and your buddy are friends. You both tell it like it is, huh?"

"The truth will set you free." She laughed. "Okay, so maybe not as free as you are right now."

I laughed and pointed to the building coming up on our left. "My dorm's right up there."

"Oh, yeah? Sabrina and I live right behind you."

"Sabrina? That's your friend's name?"

My driver laughed. "You didn't know her name?"

I shook my head.

"So, the two of you have been pushing each other's buttons since you met and you're just learning her name? That's hysterical."

"I call her Ice Queen. It seems to fit."

"Yeah, maybe with you. But she's actually pretty awesome if you get to know her."

"If you're forgetting, she left me naked and tied to a tree in the middle of the night."

"She said you were mean."

"I was fucking cold."

She laughed, but the memory churned my insides.

I'd been through hell that night. Humiliated. Overpowered. Pushed too far. "I'm not here to make friends. I've got a pro contract with my name on it and then I'm outta here."

She pulled her truck to a stop in front of my dorm and turned to look at me. "A word to the wise. Everyone needs friends."

Not in the mood to be lectured by some chick, I pushed open the passenger door. "Thanks for the ride. And the blanket."

A sad smile flashed across her face as she glanced to the blanket wrapped around me. "You can give that back after Thanksgiving. We're in room 325."

I tried to ignore the hollow in my chest as I stepped out of the truck. I'd put Thanksgiving out of my mind since I knew what I'd be doing over the long holiday weekend and it sucked. I glanced back to my driver. "Thanks again."

"Finlay," she said.

"What?"

"My name's Finlay."

I nodded my understanding and closed the door. I watched Finlay drive off before strolling to my dorm like I didn't have a blanket tied around my damned waist.

CHAPTER SEVEN

Sabrina

"Could you pass the gravy?" Finlay asked her mom across the dining room table.

Her mom held out the gravy boat, but passed it to me instead of Finlay. "Guests first," she said.

Finlay rolled her eyes as I accepted the gravy.

"Then I should get it first," Caden said from Finlay's opposite side.

"Best friends before boyfriends," I assured him. "Especially after what I caught you two doing last week."

"*Sabrina*?" Finlay said with wide eyes.

"What?" I feigned innocence. "I caught you cutting class and binge-watching *Outlander*. What'd you think I meant?" I leaned forward and winked at Caden.

Finlay's parents laughed. They got my humor. And they'd been kind enough to have Caden and me over for Thanksgiving. He was from California and wasn't going home, and it didn't make sense for me to drive to Florida for a day or two and have to drive back. I was already heading home for Christmas, so my parents were fine with me staying at Finlay's.

"So, we know how Finlay's and Caden's semesters are going. How about yours?" Mr. Thatcher said to me.

"As you'd expect. I'm pulling straight A's in my classes and beating off guys with a stick in my free time."

A deep belly laugh rumbled out of him, and my heart soared. They'd lost Finlay's twin brother, Cole, a few years ago leaving a void a mile wide in their home—especially at the holidays. I was pretty sure that's why Finlay liked having me home with her when she visited. I added the comic relief they needed to distract them from what was missing.

"She's not kidding," Caden said. "I figured Sabrina for a football girl, but she's got hockey players lined up for her."

I cocked my head and glared at Caden.

"What? Am I lying?" He winked purposefully.

"She's been out with one and the other just drives her crazy," Finlay said, clearly having her boyfriend's back and paying me back for my comment.

"She left him tied to a tree," Caden added.

"*Sabrina*," Mr. Thatcher admonished.

I shrugged. "The guy had it coming."

Mrs. Thatcher looked to me with those same thoughtful green eyes Finlay had. I braced myself for the kind-hearted lecture inevitably awaiting me. "Finlay's dad and I didn't like each other at first."

"We didn't?" Mr. Thatcher asked.

We laughed as Mrs. Thatcher's head tilted. "Remember Amber?"

"Oh." He grimaced. "Amber."

"Yes, oh Amber," Mrs. Thatcher said.

Finlay reached for a dinner roll. "Who's Amber?"

"Story for another day," Mr. Thatcher said, grabbing his own roll and stuffing it in his mouth.

"Nice save," Mrs. Thatcher said to her husband before looking to me. "All I'm saying is sometimes first impressions can be wrong."

"Nope. My first impression was dead on," I said, pushing around a piece of turkey on my plate.

"Says who?" Finlay asked.

I glared at my *friend*. "Whose side are you on?"

"I want you to be happy," she said.

"I appreciate that. But I don't think some arrogant hockey player is gonna be the one to make me happy."

"Why? Some arrogant football player makes our daughter happy," Mr. Thatcher said.

Everyone, except Caden, laughed.

Finlay's laughter slowly subsided as she looked to me, suddenly giving the impression something was wrong. "I wasn't going to say anything…"

"What?" I asked, almost nervous for her response.

"I gave Crosby a ride home the other day."

My head shot back. "What? Why?"

"Apparently, he's into public nudity."

My face fell as a sinking feeling turned my stomach. "What happened?"

"He was in a jockstrap. And nothing else," she explained.

I cringed. "Oh, no."

"Why were you alone with a guy in his jockstrap?" Caden asked jealously.

I placed my fork down on my plate and tried like hell not to feel sorry for Crosby.

Crosby

Most people spent Thanksgiving eating turkey and all the fixings with their families. Those with relatives far away might've spent it with friends. I spent mine at a federal penitentiary in Texas. Scratch that. The waiting room of a federal penitentiary in Texas after an eight-hour bus ride. Luckily, my parents' lawyer paid or else I wouldn't have been able to afford it.

I'd never had a job. Never had a reason to. My parents bought me everything I needed. They wanted me to focus on hockey, anxious for a son who played professional hockey as much as I wanted to play in the pros.

Now, everything had changed.

I'd spent the majority of the bus ride searching for a campus job—since I had no car. Most available jobs were during the day and in administrative offices. But given my class schedule during the day and my hockey schedule filling most of my nights and weekends, my availability was limited. One listing that caught my eye was for a position lasting solely for Christmas break working security in the psychology building. Since I had no home to go to and would be one of very few students remaining on campus over break, I submitted an online application and hoped for the best.

"Parks," a guard called from behind a thick glass window.

I jumped to my feet and approached the window.

"You have thirty minutes. Keep your hands on the table at all times. No touching."

I nodded.

He ticked his head to the right. "Go stand at that door and a guard will escort you in."

I nodded again and moved to the door.

Within minutes, it opened and a guard stood there. His eyes moved over my khaki pants and plain white T-shirt. I wore no shoes; they were stored in a locker with my phone and the little money I had. "Follow the rules and you won't have any problems."

I nodded and followed him to an empty table in the center of the room. Some prisoners already sat at other tables with their guests.

The guard pointed to a chair attached to the table. "Sit there."

I slipped onto the seat and folded my hands on the table, my heart suddenly thrashing around in my chest. It had only been a few weeks since I'd been there last—saying goodbye before leaving for Alabama, but every time I visited, it was a stark reminder of how my life had changed in such a definitive way.

"Like the sticks."

My eyes jumped back to the guard who still hovered beside me. "What?"

He nodded at my arm. "The hockey sticks."

I glanced down at one of the thirty tattoos on my arms. I knew the one he referred to. It had been one of my first. Two hockey sticks crisscrossed on my right forearm. "Thanks."

"You any good?"

In no mood to shoot the shit with him, I shrugged.

"Well, for what it's worth, your mother thinks you are." A small smile pulled at his lips before he walked away leaving me with a pit in my stomach.

This wasn't the life I was supposed to have. This wasn't where my mother was supposed to end up.

"Crosby?"

My eyes lifted.

My mother approached. Her once impeccably-styled hair was now graying and pulled up in a messy ponytail. Her brand-name clothes had been replaced with a prison-issued blue jumpsuit. Slip-on sneakers replaced her thousand dollar heels. And her diamond tennis bracelet my dad had given her on their first anniversary was now a pair of silver handcuffs. The whole scene was still a shock to my system.

She slipped into the seat across from me, frailer than I recalled. She managed a small smile, though tears glazed her blue eyes. "Happy Thanksgiving."

I forced my own smile. "Happy Thanksgiving."

She placed her hands on the table like mine.

I tried to avoid looking at them because all I saw were the handcuffs.

"How's school?"

I shrugged. "I'm getting used to it."

"Do you love it in Alabama?" she asked.

"It's not bad."

She closed her eyes and a look of nostalgia swept over her features. "I bet the trees have changed colors and the whole campus is filled with hues of orange and yellow."

"It is."

"And how about the buildings?" she asked. "Are the old ones with their stone pillars still as impressive as ever?"

"They are."

She opened her eyes. "Some of my best memories happened on that campus. I loved it there."

I nodded. She'd conveyed her love for Alabama hundreds of times over the years. Especially when the time came for me to decide where I'd attend college. Much to her dismay, I chose Texas. But as I sat there in a prison on Thanksgiving, staring across the table at my once vivacious mother, I could see how much she missed her freedom and the outside world.

"I want that for you," she said. "I want that campus to bring you as much joy as it brought me."

I nodded, unable to tell her what I'd been dealing with. I was there to make *her* happy. Keep *her* positive. Not complain about my shit.

"Have you spoken to your father?" she asked.

I shook my head.

She nodded. "He's got his own demons to contend with, I guess."

"Yeah." I hated him for what he'd done to her. She'd sworn up and down she had no knowledge of what he'd been doing. And I believed her. Because if she'd known, she would've tried to stop him. *And,* she never would have been foolish enough to allow him to put her name on everything. Because in the end, her name on all the paperwork is what got her convicted right along with him.

Her eyes lit up, though the lines around them appeared deeper. "How's hockey?"

"I scored a couple goals already."

She shook her head, in that proud sort of way only a mother could. "You're going pro. I just know it."

"Maybe."

"Keep playing like you've always played and the scouts won't be able to resist. Just don't give them a reason not to want you." Guilt flitted across her face. "*Another* reason for them not to want you."

"Stop blaming yourself. My skills speak for themselves. Who my parents are doesn't matter to them."

Her eyes dropped to the handcuffs on her wrists. "Let's hope."

"I'm serious."

She nodded, but I knew she didn't believe me.

"I sent some money to Rosa," I said.

Her eyes lifted to mine. "You did?"

I nodded. "I wanted her to be able to get her kid a little something for Christmas."

"Oh, honey." She reached across the table and placed her hands down on mine.

My gaze wandered to the guard who quickly looked away, as if he noticed, but wanted to give us a minute.

"I figured sending money now would give her time to find something nice. And use her coupons." A quiet laugh escaped me. "Remember how she used to spend all her free time cutting coupons?"

My mother smiled sadly, likely remembering our housekeeper. The one who'd been there for me when my parents traveled. The one who carted me to most of my practices when I was a kid and had been there for every big milestone in my life.

I called her from time to time to check that she and her new baby were doing okay. She assured me they were, but there was no way her office job paid anything like my parents had.

"That was very generous of you, but you must be depleting what little money you have left."

I shrugged. "I'll be fine. I applied for a job."

"Oh, yeah?" Her voice drifted as she removed her hands from mine. "Your father and I did you a disservice by not forcing you to make your own money." Tears rolled down her cheeks. She lifted her linked hands and wiped them away.

"It's all right. I wasn't ready for a job then. I am now."

"Right," she said, laughing through her tears. "You need money to take out all the girls who are undoubtedly fighting for your attention."

I laughed. "Obviously."

She laughed again, and I was so damn happy her tears had subsided. I hadn't visited to make her sad. Her eyes moved to my tattoos. "You haven't gotten any more, have you?"

I shook my head.

She lifted her chin at the un-tatted area on the inside of my left bicep. "Glad to see that spot's still empty."

I scoffed. "Yeah. I can assure you, it'll stay that way for a very long time."

She remained silent. I let the silence between us settle, giving her a chance to say whatever it was she wanted to say. That's how it usually worked when we spoke. She spent so much time alone, she liked having me there, whether in person or on the phone. I figured the silence was easier with someone else sharing it.

I glanced around the room at the other people. Some smiled, some cried. It wasn't a happy place by any means. It reminded you that you were separated from the people you loved. And no matter how terrible their crime, they still loved you.

"I think you should talk to someone."

My eyes shot back to my mom. "What?"

"I've been talking to someone in here. You know, to help me…adjust. She thinks you could benefit from talking to someone too. Someone to work through your anger."

"You think I'm angry?"

She tilted her head. Instantly, I was transported to her standing in our kitchen, giving me the same look when she didn't believe what I was telling her. "It would be alarming if you weren't."

I dragged my teeth over my bottom lip, unsure what to say. Of course, I was angry. I had a million reasons to be.

"My counselor looked into it for me," she continued. "The campus has a counseling center. All you have to do is schedule an appointment."

I didn't know if I should've been angry she thought I had anger issues—yes, I see the irony there—or if I should've felt fortunate that even behind bars, she thought about me and wanted what was best for me. "I'll think about it."

She nodded. "Thank you. That's all I wanted…I love you, Crosby."

"I love you too."

CHAPTER EIGHT

Sabrina

"Nice seats," Finlay said as she glanced behind us at the arena filled with fans. "But why front row?" Her head twisted back around and her eyes cut to mine. "I thought you weren't into Jeremy?"

I shrugged. "I told him I'd check out a game."

"That the only reason?"

"What's that supposed to mean?" I asked.

"Just saying there are other guys on the team besides Jeremy."

I rolled my eyes.

"You heard what my mom said."

I opened my mouth to stop her from going all Team Crosby on me, but the lights lowered and strobe lights and loud music filled the arena.

People stood as both hockey teams were introduced. The crowd erupted into applause and shouts as the players took to the ice, skating big wide circles around the rink with fierce speed.

I glanced behind me, realizing hockey fans were just as energetic as football fans when it came to cheering on their favorite players.

Once the lights switched back on, the teams took their sides of the ice and shot at their empty nets. Jeremy took a shot, turned, and skated by us. Catching sight of us, he circled back around and lifted his gloved hand as he passed by. I smiled as I sat back down in my seat.

"Not seeing gaga eyes," Finlay said as she sat down beside me.

I kept my eyes on the ice. Jeremy passed the puck back and forth with one of his teammates as he moved closer to the empty net once again, burying the puck in the back of it with ease.

Finlay jumped to her feet and banged on the glass in front of us.

"What are you doing?" I asked.

She turned to me and winked.

On the ice, Crosby glanced to her, lifting his head in recognition, before his eyes cut to mine, narrowing on sight.

He did *not* just glare at me. I lifted my hand and flipped him off.

"Sabrina," Finlay chided.

Crosby laughed. The asshole laughed again as he skated off.

Finlay shook her head. "I've never seen anyone get to you the way he does."

"It's called hate."

She shrugged. "It beats that indifferent thing you do."

I considered arguing, but what was the point. She was right. I had indifferent down. It's what I did. It's how I kept my feelings in check. I was no different than anyone else. I'd had my heart broken and broken my fair share of hearts. Just because I wasn't in a rush to open my heart to some unworthy college guy, it didn't make me strange. It made me smart. No one wanted to be hurt, and letting people in was a sure-fire way to do that. That's why I kept my small circle close, and I wore indifference well.

My eyes shifted back to the ice where the players from both teams lined up at center ice. Everyone around me stood. I watched Crosby. Watched the way his eyes remained on the flag hanging from the rafters as the National Anthem echoed through the arena. The guys on either side of him had treated him like crap, and yet, there he stood. A virtual 'fuck you' to all of them.

Why was hockey so important to him? Why had he allowed himself to be fodder for the immature idiots on the team? It seemed so unlike the guy I'd become familiar with to put up with other people's shit. I would've envisioned him as someone who took on the entire team alone as opposed to someone who bowed down and played dead. But that's exactly what he'd been doing. There had to be more to it. And I wondered if it had anything to do with why he ended up in Alabama.

Once the last note of the National Anthem drifted through the speakers, the game began and players flew by us. The slick puck slipped across the ice from stick to stick and side to side. The puck was hard to follow as it was passed around, but I tried to keep up. Jeremy, in number thirty-three, zipped by us, handling the puck effortlessly. Crosby, in number fifty-six, was a blur on the ice. The guy could move. He always seemed to be where the puck was, stopping and passing it from wherever he ended up.

Hockey was a rough sport. Much rougher than I expected. Players were shoved and knocked off their feet. But no matter how many shots the players took on the net, no goals had been scored. As it neared the end of the first period (apparently hockey had three), two players slammed into the glass right in front of us. The unexpected commotion sent me jerking back in my seat. Finlay, along with everyone around us, jumped to her feet. The crowd bellowed, yelling at the two players who tore off their gloves and went at it. Fists flew for at least a minute before the refs skated over and pulled them apart. They disengaged and skated off to what I assumed to be the penalty box.

Once the puck dropped again, it came loose and Crosby took off with it, skating down the ice with his opponents on his tail. It didn't seem to faze him as his stick shifted the puck from side to side. He circled behind the opposing team's goal. It looked like he was going to come out on the right side, but he circled back and, as if the goalie wasn't even there, he slapped the puck in the net. The buzzer sounded and the red light above the goal lit up.

The crowd cheered as Crosby punched his hands and stick in the air. In hockey movies, the teammates surrounded the scorer, embracing him and patting his helmet with their gloved hands. But on the ice, no one surrounded Crosby. They celebrated with each other, just not with him. The coaches congratulated him with pats on the back as he hopped into their team's box and dropped down onto the bench.

Finlay and I exchanged a curious look. We knew athletes. We were surrounded by them all the time. Even if the guy was a douchebag, he still scored a goal. You congratulated him. You went back to hating him after the game. Apparently, the hockey team lived by another set of rules.

"Let's go," I said.

"What?" Finlay asked

I stood from my seat and grabbed my coat. "I'm all set." And I was. I hadn't shown up to feel sorry for Crosby—yet again.

CHAPTER NINE

December

Crosby

I lay on my bed with an ice pack on my shoulder and a heating pad on my ribs, trying to ignore the bass reverberating in the room beneath mine. I had a test in economics the following day I hadn't studied for. But shutting out all the noise rattling around in my head was easier said than done.

Someone pounding on my door pulled me from my thoughts. I wasn't expecting anyone, so I ignored it. But the pounding persisted. I shoved the ice and heating pad away and rolled off my bed. I trudged to the door and yanked it open. "What?"

Sabrina stood outside my door. Her eyes shot to the number on the door then back to me. "Where's Jeremy?"

"Jeremy?"

"Yeah, he texted and said he'd be here."

My head dropped back and my shoulders shook with cold laughter. That son of a bitch.

"What's so funny?"

"This is the last place he'd be."

She folded her arms across her chest. "Then why'd he send me here?"

I shrugged. "The guy's a prick. Who knows why he does anything he does."

Her lips twisted, and my eyes were immediately drawn to them.

I hadn't realized how luscious they were. How nice they'd likely taste. *What the hell was wrong with me?* My eyes snapped up. "He probably wanted me to see that not only had he gotten you seats for our game, but he also scored another date."

"First of all, he didn't get me tickets. And why would he care if you knew he scored another date?"

"Because he's a prick."

She rolled her eyes. "Where's he live?"

"Beats the hell outta me. I'm not the one visiting him for a romp in the sack."

Her eyes widened.

Watching the irritation play out across her face tightened my balls.

"We were going to study, asshole."

I held up my hands in surrender. "Didn't mean to suggest you were that type of girl."

Her eyes narrowed. "Of course you did. You do it every time we're within a fifty-foot radius."

"Someone's been hanging on my every word."

She sucked in a sharp breath. I wouldn't have been surprised if she kicked me in the balls. I definitely deserved it. "It's hard to miss your words when you're insulting me and calling me a slut at every turn."

"The word slut never came out of my mouth."

She growled low in her throat and turned to walk away.

I reached out and grabbed her arm.

She spun back around, anger brimming in her eyes before she glared at my hand wrapped around her wrist. "Let go of me."

"I..." I dropped her wrist, realizing how desperate I looked. What the fuck did I care if I hurt her? Hurting people I could do. I could control.

"You what? Wanted to add assault to your growing list of infractions against me?"

"Infractions?" I scoffed. "What are you studying to be a lawyer or something?"

"Maybe."

I could definitely see that. The fire in her eyes. The determination in her steps. The seriousness in her tone.

"Finlay told me about the jockstrap incident. Why are you still letting those assholes get away with treating you the way they are?"

I could feel every muscle in my body tense up. Why the hell did she care? "It doesn't matter."

"Of course it matters," she said.

"You know what I can't understand?" I crossed my arms, irritated by her inquisition. "You call them assholes, but you're here to meet one of them."

Her jaw ticked. "You know what I can't understand? I can't understand why you're so hot and cold all the time. Why you came to campus in the middle of the semester. And why you're letting people do horrible things to you and you won't rat them out."

"That it?"

"I'm sure I could think of more if you gave me another minute."

I dug my hands into the pockets of my basketball shorts. What did she want to hear? The truth? Well, the truth sucked. And regardless of what I told her, it changed nothing. She was there to see captain asshole. "Well, I don't want to hold you up. I can totally see why you'd want to hang out with the prick now."

Her entire face reddened. "What's that supposed to mean?"

I looked her up and down, the same way she had me on the night we met. The thought of her and Jeremy left a rancid taste in my mouth and the only thing I wanted to do was push her away. "Attitude and desperation. Total puck bunny material."

Her eyes flared before she spun away from me.

"Hey," I called once she'd taken a few steps.

She whirled back around with daggers in her eyes. "What?"

I grabbed Finlay's blanket from the chair by my door and tossed it to her. "Give this back to Finlay."

She shot me the look of death before storming away with the blanket clenched in her hands.

This time I let her go.

Sabrina

I rounded the corner, stopping to inhale a much-needed breath. *Stupid. Stupid. Stupid.* Why had I allowed myself to feel sorry for him on Thanksgiving? Why had I allowed myself to feel sorry for him at the game? Why had I let him get to me?

Ughhhhh.

I banged the back of my head against the wall, hoping to knock some sense into myself. Why had Jeremy sent me to Crosby's room? Was it a pissing contest between the two of them? Had I been a pawn?

Crosby's words from the rink played through my mind. 'Why hasn't he asked you out before now?' *Was* I just another way to get to Crosby? But why? We barely even knew each other?

My phone pinged in my messenger bag. I dug inside and pulled it out. Speak of the devil.

Everything OK? Jeremy's text read.

Seriously? **You sent me to the wrong room.**

Shit. I did? I'm in 129.

If this *was* a game, two could play it. **No worries. You sent me to Crosby's room. Turns out he's not so bad.**

The three dots appeared and I suddenly couldn't wait to see how he'd respond. **So, when will you be here?**

Gahhh. Asshole.

Sorry. We decided to hang out. I shoved my phone into my messenger bag and took off for home.

"Guys suck," I said to Finlay as I plopped down onto my bed a few minutes later.

She glanced up from her bed where her nose was buried in her notebook. "I take it studying didn't go so well?"

"It didn't go anywhere. He sent me to Crosby's room."

Her eyes narrowed as I tossed her blanket to her. "Why?"

I fell back onto my bed and draped my arm across my eyes. "It's like he's playing some game with Crosby and I somehow got caught in the middle."

"What a jerk." There was a long pause before Finlay spoke again. "So, Crosby?"

"Stop." I was in no mood for her pro-Crosby campaign.

"Just saying. You went to his room."

"Not by choice."

"But don't you think it's the least bit interesting that you two keep running into each other?"

I removed my arm from my eyes and cut a glance her way. "Nothing about us running into each other is interesting. Exhausting, maybe. But definitely not interesting."

"He needs friends, Sabrina."

"Well, he has a shitty way of going about it."

CHAPTER TEN

Sabrina

I purposely entered class as the professor began to close the door so I wouldn't have to talk to Jeremy. I slipped into my seat and dug into my bag, avoiding eye contact.

"Hey," he whispered as the professor rattled off the directions for our test.

I didn't look his way.

"You're not talking to me now?"

I turned my head slowly and glared at him, before turning back to the front of the room where the professor distributed our tests.

"We need to talk," Jeremy whispered.

I ignored him and focused on my test. Communications I could deal with. Communicating with him, I could not.

After an hour, I heard the rustling of students turning in their tests and leaving the classroom. *Shit.* I'd only answered forty of sixty questions. I plugged away at the remaining twenty and put every bit of effort I had left into those answers. Once our professor gave the half-hour warning, I glanced around the room. Only a few people remained. Thankfully, Jeremy wasn't one of them.

With minutes to spare, I finished writing my final response. I gathered my bag and handed in my test with a mix of relief and confidence. Though it took me longer than most, it had been a lot easier than I expected. I stepped out of the classroom, eager to meet up with Finlay outside so we could grab some lunch.

"Hey," Jeremy said, jumping to his feet from where he sat on the hallway floor.

I continued walking.

"Wait," he called, catching up with me.

"What?"

"I waited for you."

"So?"

He followed me down the stairwell to the exit. "Would you stop and talk to me?"

"Why? So you can come up with some lame excuse for why you played me."

"Played you?"

When we reached the sidewalk in front of the building, I spun to face him. "How stupid do I look? I know you purposely sent me to Crosby's room."

He dug his hands into his pockets, not bothering to deny it.

"I'm not into games. So, whatever you two are playing, I want no part of it."

"I like you, Sabrina."

"I think you like making Crosby look stupid more."

He said nothing.

I walked off, not giving him a second glance.

"Whoa," Finlay said as she hurried over to me. "What was that about?"

I rolled my eyes. "He tried to explain."

"What'd he say?"

"Nothing I didn't already know. You were right about the gaga eyes. He never gave them to me."

"Say that again," Finlay said.

"What?"

"'You were right.' I love hearing you say that."

I laughed.

"Come on. Let's grab a coffee and talk crap about him."

Crosby

Xavier, our back-up forward, slid his nearly-filled cardboard box over to me. I packed my hundredth box of mashed potatoes into it before sliding it to our goalie JR, who packed the canned corn. The box ended with Jeremy who packed the pie mix.

Coach had arranged a team-building event at a local shelter helping with Christmas care packages for needy families. I loaded another box of potatoes in, passing it along while cursing the fact that we needed to keep up appearances for the coach and the workers at the shelter who were thrilled to have us helping.

"You going out with us after?" Xavier whispered as he slid the next box to me.

"Seriously?"

"It'll be fun. We never all get to let loose together."

"Oh, I think these guys let loose fine when I'm not around."

"Come on. You and me. We'll stick together."

I eyed the six-foot redhead freshman, laughing to myself that he wanted to be my wingman. It *had* been some time since I let loose with anyone. An overzealous freshman was better than no one. "Okay."

He seemed surprised. "Yeah?"

"What the hell."

He laughed and passed me another box. "You know how to dance?"

I laughed. "You asking me to dance, freshman?"

His cheeks reddened. "What? Me? No. But girls like guys who get out on the dance floor and dance."

"You looking for a girl?" I asked.

He shrugged. "Wouldn't mind one."

"Well, let's see what we can do about that then."

A smile spread across his freckled face.

If anyone asked me what I thought I'd be doing a year ago at this time, I would've said playing pro hockey—not going clubbing with a freshman who was looking to get laid. Yet, that's what the cards had in store for me. So, I did what I'd been doing since I arrived on campus. I rolled with it.

Sabrina

The music in the bar had been kicked up. The colorful lights over the dance floor flashed. One more drink and I'd be in the middle of the dance floor getting my mother-effing groove on. If anyone deserved it, I did.

"Be back with drinks," Caden said before heading to the bar and leaving Finlay and me with Forester. Apparently, Forester and his ex—who I'd pushed him back to in a moment of selflessness—had gotten back together over Thanksgiving break, and the guy hadn't stopped smiling since.

"Hey, I've been meaning to talk to you," he said in that smooth way he did everything.

I waited, unsure what he could possibly need to say to me.

"I never thanked you for your advice at my party." His blue eyes practically twinkled and his damn dimples dug into his cheeks. Did the guy have to be so hot?

"No need to thank me. It was obvious what you needed to do. Besides, I'm a sucker for a happy ending."

He wrapped an arm around my shoulders and pulled me into him, dropping a kiss on the crown of my head like a big brother would do. "I owe you one."

"Think any of your men will be here?" Finlay asked, interrupting our moment.

Forester's arm dropped away from my shoulders, and I wished it hadn't left me feeling bereft. "Men?"

I rolled my eyes. "My friend is clearly buzzed and doesn't know when to zip it."

He glanced back to Finlay, waiting for her to fill in the blanks.

She zipped her lips like a little kid would do and tossed away the imaginary key. The girl wasn't a big drinker, so any alcohol affected her. Usually, it was cute. Tonight, when she was drawing attention to me, not so much.

A flicker of concern flashed across Forester's face. "Someone fucking with you?"

"Retract the claws macho football player," I laughed. "I can protect myself."

He smirked. "Says the little spitfire."

"I'm not little."

Finlay and Forester exchanged a knowing look before I turned away from them and checked out the dance floor. Couples swayed to the slow song filtering through the speakers.

My thoughts reeled me back to the last time I'd been there. I'd thought something might happen between Forester and me. The way he held me on the dance floor. The way he stared into my eyes. The way he made me feel. Now I knew he hadn't been seeing me at all. He'd been trying to get over his ex.

Ugh. I was so pathetic.

I could feel someone standing beside me.

"Hey. I didn't know you'd be here," he drawled.

I turned to my left. Jeremy stood there. I didn't even bother trying to hide my disgust. "Why would you?"

"You're still mad." The guy was a lot of things, but he clearly knew a disgusted female when he saw one.

"Not mad. Just nothing."

"Look—"

"No, you look," I said. "You clearly have something you're holding over Crosby to make him put up with your immature crap."

"Says who?"

"Why don't you leave him alone?"

"You don't understand."

"You're right. I don't. Maybe the dean will."

"Be smart, Sabrina," he warned, his tone hardened and his eyes all wide and scary. "You wouldn't want to start something you don't know how to stop."

"This one of 'em?" Forester said, pulling my attention away from Jeremy.

Jeremy reached in front of me and held his fist out to bump Forester's—as if he hadn't just threatened me. "Hey, Trace Forester. Nice to meet you, man."

Forester didn't reciprocate, looking to me instead. "You need me to get rid of him?"

I didn't know what to say. I'd witnessed a scary version of Jeremy and it unsettled me to see how quickly it appeared then disappeared.

"I don't know what she told you," Jeremy said to Forester. "But you've got it all wrong."

"No, dude," Caden said, purposely pushing between Jeremy and me as he stepped back to the table balancing multiple shots and our round of beers in his hands. "*You've* got it all wrong. She doesn't want to be bothered tonight. She's out with friends."

Jeremy glanced to me.

I spun my stool away from him and grabbed a shot, downing it like the rock star I was. Or, at least, the rock star I told myself I was.

"What's his deal?" Forester asked once Jeremy walked away.

"We went out once, then he pulled a jerk move and sent me to the room of a guy he hates."

"Crosby's room," Finlay interjected.

"Who's Crosby?" Forester asked.

I grabbed another shot and downed it, wincing at the potency of its after bite.

"Tree boy," Caden said.

"She calls him Mr. Hockey," Finlay added. "And he calls her Ice Queen. It's adorable."

"So, tree boy plays hockey?" Forester asked, trying to make sense of the information being thrown at him.

I nodded, gradually feeling the warming effects of the shots. "He's actually pretty good."

"He's going pro," Finlay added.

My eyes shot to hers. "How do you know that?"

"He told me."

Forester's phone buzzed on the table. His face lit up as he stepped off his stool and excused himself to take the call outside where he'd be able to hear who I assumed to be his girlfriend Marin on the other end.

"Someone's whipped," Caden said.

Finlay knocked her shoulder into his. "I think it's cute."

"I think you're cute," Caden said.

I rolled my eyes at their corniness, but deep down I knew how great they were together. And if anyone deserved to be happy, it was Finlay. It had taken her a long time to join the land of the living again after her brother died. Now she had an awesome boyfriend who adored her and a friend like me who was simply amazing.

"Why aren't you dancing?" a familiar voice asked me.

I didn't even need to look this time. I knew it was Crosby. And I knew the underlying challenge in his voice. "Finlay, did you say something?" I asked.

Her eyes stayed on Crosby who stood beside me as she shook her head, stifling a smile.

Caden laughed. "Sorry, Sabrina. It wasn't me neither."

Though I hadn't looked over, I could feel Crosby's nearness and smell his woodsy scent. "Well, I only have the stomach for football players tonight. If I see another hockey player, I may be inclined to show my claws."

Crosby leaned closer, speaking into my ear. "Looks like we've got a problem then. Because I'd love to see your claws."

"You want me to get rid of him," Caden asked, suddenly acting all tough and protective.

But all I needed was a bar brawl to break out on my behalf. A long, frustrated whoosh left my lips before I swiveled to face Crosby.

A dark short-sleeved shirt clung to his ripped arms and chest, his tattoos there for the world to see. His backward hat covered his black hair but made his light blue eyes stand out in the dark bar. He looked good. *Damn* good.

Shiiiiit.

The alcohol was clearly messing with my brain. "What do you want?"

A crooked smile pulled his lips up on one side. "Oh, there're a lot of things I want. But here, I think dancing would be the only acceptable option."

My eyes flared. "Sounds like more insinuations that I'm a slut who'd let you do dirty things to me."

"Again, the word slut never left my lips. Nor did the word dirty—though I'd totally be up for it."

I growled.

He leaned in closer, clearly not deterred by my growing annoyance with him. "I like when you purr."

"That was a growl," I snapped, hating that my exasperation was mixing with a slightly-buzzed attraction to him.

"Semantics."

"Stop!" I said.

"Stop what?"

"This split personality thing. I can't keep up with which Crosby I'm getting. Either you think I'm a bitch or you realize how freaking amazing I am. Either you think I'm a slut or you've figured out I'm a strong confident woman. You need to pick one."

"I don't need to do anything."

My hands bunched into fists. "See? This is why I can't deal with you."

"Are you gonna dance with me or not?"

"Not."

He snickered, seemingly amused. "Why not?"

"Because whether you hate me or like me, I hate you," I assured him.

"Hate's a strong word."

"So are bitch and slut."

"Never called you a slut and the only reason I called you a bitch is because you left me tied to a tree."

"You didn't appreciate my help."

"Go dance with him," Finlay called across the table.

What the hell? My wide eyes moved to hers. The traitor winked.

Crosby leaned closer. "Your friend can see you want me."

"Dude, persistence is good," Caden said. "But lose the arrogance. Sabrina's not the type of girl to go for it."

"Thank you, Caden."

"And I wasn't saying she wants you," Finlay added. "I wanted her to have fun. Any chump would've done."

Crosby burst out laughing. "Any chump, huh?" He glanced to me. "So, you in?"

My shoulders dropped. *What. The. Hell?* "Will you leave me alone after?"

"Depends."

"On what?"

"Will you be able to leave *me* alone after?"

A laugh shot out of me. The guy was delusional. "Oh, I assure you. That will not be a problem."

He stepped back so I could get off my stool. "Prove it."

"Watch me." I hopped down and made my way to the crowded dance floor. By the time I reached it, one of my favorite songs played. My hips swayed and my arms moved above my head as I felt the beat deep inside me pounding away.

Crosby stepped up behind me. His hands landed on my hips. They were strong and steadying and moving right along with the sway of my body. I relaxed, allowing myself to keep pace with the music despite his close proximity. The bass in the song resounded inside my body, thumping in tandem with my heart.

I hated that it felt normal to be dancing with him. That I wasn't resisting. That I was being weak and disregarding how he treated me. How he acted. All I knew was I had this strong guy holding onto me and he knew how to dance. He knew how to move his body.

The hard plains of his chest pressed against my back, and I relaxed even more, my head dropping against his shoulder. That's when I felt the hard length of his erection pressing against my ass.

Shit, shit, shiiiiit.

I tried to resist. Tried to stop myself from succumbing to the alcohol coursing through my veins. But my efforts were futile. I pushed back into it. The tingles zinging between my thighs came fast. It was exciting and frustrating all at the same time. The guy I hated could *not* be the one to awaken my body.

His fingers, still spread on my hips, slipped around to my stomach. I wanted to fight it. Wanted to step away from him. But the hum of my body wouldn't allow it. He lowered his head, burying his nose into my neck. "You smell amazing."

Though my thighs quivered, I tried to remain indifferent. "It's called sweat."

He laughed. "Well, then I'd like nothing more than to taste your sweat."

The thought of his lips on my neck sent a delicious shiver rocking through me. "Do lines like that normally work for you?"

"Who said it's a line?"

His hands slipped under the hem of my shirt and coasted across my bare stomach. "God, you feel so good."

"You're a horny guy. Of course I do."

He shook his head, his nose running along my jawline. "I may be horny, but you still feel right in my arms. I'm wondering how you'd feel beneath me."

I jerked away from his grasp, spinning to face him. "That." I jammed my finger into his chest. "That right there is why this was a bad idea." The traitorous hum of my body persisted as the lights flashed across his confused face. "It's like you're capable of being normal for like two minutes then you turn into an asshole. I don't get it. And I'm over it." I turned away from him and pushed through the crowd to get back to the table.

Finlay's eyes told me she'd seen my abrupt departure. She jumped down from her stool and grabbed Caden's hand. "Let's go."

I picked up my beer and downed it.

"Wait," Crosby said from behind me.

Caden stepped up in Crosby's face, pressing his hand into his chest. "We're leaving. You're not."

"Dude," Crosby said.

Forester returned to the table and draped his arm around my shoulder, spinning me away from Crosby. "I leave you alone for a few minutes and all hell breaks loose. You okay?"

"Yeah," I said. "Just another guy being a jerk."

"I take great offense to that," Forester teased as we walked outside the bar, leaving the music and people behind us.

I leaned my body against the outside wall of the bar, as we waited for Caden and Finlay to get the car. "You're one of the last good ones, Forester."

"Go on," he said with his signature smirk.

I rolled my eyes.

"You'll find someone."

I cocked my head. "You make me sound desperate."

He shook his head. "Nope. You're just too good for most of the guys on campus, that's all."

I laughed, knowing he was only trying to make me feel better, but it helped. At least until my next encounter with Crosby. The guy had a way of driving me freaking nuts. And what was up with my body's response to his touch and the words he uttered against my skin?

I had a sinking feeling deep down in my bones that my knee-jerk reaction and quick departure had nothing to do with what he'd said, and everything to do with self-preservation.

Damn him.

CHAPTER ELEVEN

Crosby

The past week had been balls to the walls. With practices, games, and cramming for final exams, I'd barely had time to breathe. I'd taken my literature final that morning—the last one before Christmas break, and endured my final practice until our January twelfth game in Tennessee. I walked back to my dorm from the arena with exhaustion weighing me down.

I spotted Sabrina opening the trunk of her car in front of her dorm. I hadn't seen her since the night at the bar. And to say our interaction had been fucked up would've been an understatement. She'd been feeling me and *definitely* grinding up on me. But then she went and got all whacked out over me flirting with her. She had to know I was kidding around. Though, let's be honest. Had she said, 'Let's take it back to my place,' I would've been all in.

I ground to a halt on the sidewalk and watched as she packed a bag of wrapped presents into her trunk. Did I say something to her or would it be safer to bypass her dorm altogether? Maybe I could wish her a merry Christmas and show her I wasn't the asshole she thought I was. It wasn't like we'd see each other for another month anyway.

Fuck it.

"Hey," I called to her.

She pulled her head out from around her raised trunk. She rolled her eyes as soon as she spotted me then went back to packing.

I stepped up beside her car. "How's it going?"

"That's what you want to know?"

I shrugged. "Seemed like a legitimate question."

"I'm great." She slammed the trunk and walked to the passenger side, loading her carry-on bag into the front seat.

Most guys would've taken the hint and gotten the hell outta there, but I wasn't most guys. "I haven't seen you in a while."

"Yup. It's been great," she said.

"You've been avoiding me?"

"Nope. I just think the stars aligned."

Even when she was pissing me off I found humor in it. "So, you heading home?"

"I'm certainly not packing for fun."

What the hell was it gonna take? I buried my hands in my pockets. "I liked dancing with you."

She finally stopped what she was doing and glanced over at me. "We danced?"

I laughed. "Funny."

Her eyes narrowed. "When?"

"Stop fucking around. You know we danced at the bar."

She shrugged. "I was wasted. It must've not been that memorable."

I deep growl came out of me. Apparently, she was pissing me off more than I realized. "What's it gonna take?"

She dug her hands into her hips. "What?"

"Us? This thing we keep doing. When are we getting past it?"

Her head tilted to the side. "Maybe when I meet the real you."

I threw my hands out to my sides. "What the hell's that supposed to mean?"

She slammed the passenger door and circled the front of the car. "I told you. I never know what I'm getting with you. From the first time we met until the bar, you've got my head spinning."

"So, you do remember the bar."

She pulled open her driver's side door with vigor. "Are you not even hearing me?"

"I hear you."

"Until you're normal for more than two minutes, we're nothing to each other." She slid into the driver's seat and pulled the door closed.

"Merry fucking Christmas," I said to her car as it pulled away from the sidewalk and disappeared from view.

CHAPTER TWELVE

Sabrina

Growing up in Florida, I'd never experienced fragrant pine covering homes and buildings. I'd never woken up to a dusting of snow on Christmas morning. I'd never even had a real Christmas tree. One day, I'd venture up north. One day, I'd escape the heat of Florida. For now, the illuminated palm trees lining the streets of my neighborhood would have to do.

"Watch it!" my best friend Trish shouted at the car that pulled out in front of us.

Her exaggerated impatience pulled my attention from the familiar streets of my childhood.

Trish had been my best friend since junior high. But we'd lost touch while I'd been in Alabama and she'd stayed home to attend community college. But once we got together in the same place, it was as if we'd never been apart. We still laughed at the same jokes. Still found the same guys hot. Still turned heads when we entered rooms.

"I wanna see you hook up with Steve tonight," she said, her eyes jumping between the road and me in her passenger seat.

"Not gonna happen," I assured her.

"Why not? You said you're not seeing anyone at school."

"I'm not, but it doesn't mean I need a one-night-stand with my ex. He's my ex for a reason."

She laughed. "I bet he has an amazing tan. Can you even imagine going to college in Hawaii?"

I shook my head, though I could totally see Steve living the life there.

We entered the party and were greeted by so many familiar faces. We bee-lined it for the kitchen to grab a drink. Before I knew it, Trish and I were pulled in opposite directions. All the guys wanted to talk Bama football with me, as usual. They knew my bestie at school was dating the quarterback, so they figured I had insight into how the team would do if they made it to the championship game.

"Sabrina," Trish called impatiently from the kitchen a little while later.

"One minute," I said to her. I was deep in conversation with a girl from high school who was attending college in New Hampshire. Not only did I want to hear about her time there, I didn't like being beckoned.

Trish rolled her eyes and went back to mixing drinks at the kitchen island. I'd forgotten how possessive she was over me. She never liked me veering away from our group. But never one to follow anyone—or much less care what anyone thought, I always did my own thing.

I finished my conversation, got myself a drink, and spotted Trish outside hanging with a small group of people we'd graduated with. Most of them went to school out of state, so opportunities like these were our chance to get back together and catch up.

I grabbed hold of the back door handle, eager to join my old friends outside.

"Sabrina."

I knew that voice immediately. I dropped the door handle and spun around. Steve stood there looking as hot as he had when we'd dated—all tall, blond, and tanned. Even in high school, we were mature enough to admit we didn't belong together. I was the girl with a comeback for everything. He was the guy who loved my comebacks but loved other girls just as much. "Hey."

He walked up to me and pulled me into a hug. "When'd you get home?"

"Late last night. You?" I stepped out of his arms.

"Flew in a couple days ago."

I nodded. "How's Hawaii treating you? Must be torture."

He laughed. "Surf instructor by day, student by night. Not a bad gig."

I laughed, picturing the heads turning as he walked shirtless down the beach. "I bet."

His eyes perused me slowly. "You're looking good."

"Obviously."

He laughed as he glanced around. "Who you with?"

"Trish. She's outside."

"So, you didn't bring a boyfriend home with you?"

I shook my head. "Do you think any Bama boy could handle all this?"

He burst out laughing as he wrapped his arm around my shoulders and pulled me into his side. "I've missed you." He pushed open the back door, and we stepped outside onto the brick patio together.

The mild December night air hit us as we approached Trish whose back faced us. The people she stood with noticed Steve and me and their eyes widened. Did they think we were back together?

"She's changed since she's been in Alabama," Trish told the group. "Was she this much of a bitch before she left? Or was I just too busy being one of her minions to notice?"

Steve's hand tightened on my shoulder, knowing I'd be reeling from her harsh words.

"Hey, Sabrina," a girl standing beside Trish said, attempting to shut her up. But I'd heard enough to know where I stood with my old friend.

Trish turned quickly, her guilty eyes on me.

The only sound on that silent patio was a firetruck's siren bellowing in the distance.

I hoped my anger carried through my eyes as I stared at Trish, all the good times we'd shared vanishing as if in a cloud of smoke. "Being someone's minion is a choice," I said. "I never asked you to be anything but my friend. Clearly, that was too difficult for you." I pulled free from Steve's grasp, looking to him briefly. "It was nice to see you."

He nodded sadly as I turned and walked back through the house and right out the front door.

* * *

My family began arriving at one on Christmas day. That was my cue to head downstairs from my bedroom to greet them. I'd only been home for a couple days, but as much as I loved seeing my parents, I missed being on campus with Finlay—my real friend.

I heard Aunt Pat's voice before I even reached the foyer. Her larger-than-life personality commanded an audience whenever she entered a room. My cousin Sasha, her only daughter, always seemed to fade into the background when her mother was around. I wondered how she was doing away at college. She'd been eager to get away from home, opting for school in Texas as opposed to Florida. I wondered if she'd shed her shyness and come out of her shell while away.

I bounded down the stairs in my red dress and shimmery heels, careful of the banisters wrapped with greenery and lights. My parents greeted Aunt Pat and Sasha in the foyer. Though it was sixty degrees outside, Aunt Pat donned a fur coat. Sasha looked good. Happier. Her jeans and red cashmere top was such a change from the frumpy clothes she used to wear. And her usual brunette bob had grown out and now hung in bouncy waves.

"Merry Christmas," I said, greeting them both with hugs.

Sasha's face lit up. "Merry Christmas."

"Why don't you get me a drink," Aunt Pat said to my dad, her voice echoing off the cathedral ceiling. "Something nice and strong."

I glanced to Sasha who rolled her eyes. I ticked my head toward the stairs and she followed me up to my room.

I sat down on the edge of my bed, while Sasha walked around, looking at all the pictures I tucked under the crisscrossed ribbons on my photo boards. Most were old high school photos I hadn't bothered to replace yet. But some were of Finlay and me, in our room or with Caden after his football games.

"How's Texas?" I asked.

Sasha spun around, her wide giddy eyes saying it all. "Amazing. I've made so many friends."

"That's great."

"Yeah," she sighed with a contentedness I wasn't used to seeing in her.

I lifted a brow. "Any guys?"

She smiled. "Apparently, I'm a sucker for thick southern accents."

I tossed back my head and laughed, knowing exactly what she meant. Those fuck-me drawls melted their fair share of panties on my campus, too. "Be careful. They know how much we love them so they lay them on thicker."

She laughed, before sitting down beside me. "Can I ask you something?"

"Of course."

"Is it just me or does it feel weird being home for you?"

"No, it feels weird," I agreed, the recent encounter with Trish leaving a bitter taste in my mouth.

"It's like everyone changes."

"And not necessarily for the better," I added.

"Agreed."

I smiled. "Of course you agree. Great minds and all."

We laughed and talked more before joining my parents and Aunt Pat in the dining room a little while later. The table was filled with every food imaginable. My parents always put out a huge spread—regardless of the number of guests we entertained.

Aunt Pat dominated the conversation as usual, and more than once did I bite my lip to stop from laughing at my parents rolling their eyes at each other.

"How's school, Sabrina?" Aunt Pat asked right as I'd bitten into my beef tenderloin.

I nodded my response as I chewed down my meat.

"We're just waiting for final grades to be posted," my mom answered for me. "But Sabrina's confident she passed all her classes."

"Just passed?" Aunt Pat asked, aghast.

"Yup. Passing works for us," my dad said with a smile.

I smiled across the table at him and he winked back at me.

"Well, despite all the hoopla that happened on Sasha's campus, she's still earning straight A's," Aunt Pat said, taking a long draught of her glass of wine.

"Congratulations, Sasha," my mom said.

Sasha smiled, clearly appreciating my mom's kindness despite her own mother's frankness.

"What hoopla are you referring to?" my dad asked.

Sasha opened her mouth to explain, but Aunt Pat cut her off. "The whole Parks scandal."

My mom tilted her head. "Parks scandal?"

"That Texas couple who'd been embezzling millions of dollars from their investors for years."

My mother shrugged. "Guess we missed it."

"It was all over the news," Aunt Pat said. "When people wanted to cash out their investments, their earnings had been substantially lower than expected. They started asking questions and it became this huge scandal. People lost millions of dollars. Families lost homes. Companies went bankrupt."

"So, what's that have to do with Sasha?" my dad asked.

Sasha opened her mouth to explain, but Aunt Pat cut her off again. "Their boy went to Sasha's school. Big time hockey player."

My ears pricked up at the mention of a hockey player.

"Camera crews were camped out on campus," Sasha explained. "The poor guy couldn't go anywhere without reporters hounding him. He finally up and disappeared."

"Geez," my dad said.

My eyes bounced between Sasha and Aunt Pat. "Where'd he go?"

Sasha shrugged. "His parents were sent to prison, and no one's been repaid the money that was stolen from them. So, there are a lot of angry people out there. Seems his parents were trying to keep him away from those determined to get what was owed to them."

The thumping in my heart told me what I already knew. "What's his name?"

"Crosby," Sasha said. "Crosby Parks."

I choke-coughed.

My dad handed me a glass of water. "You okay?"

I waved him off as I looked to Sasha. "You've got to be kidding me."

Sasha's eyes expanded, brimming with intrigue. "Do you know him?"

I pulled in a deep breath, finally understanding why Crosby ended up at my school. Why he was so angry. Why his mood changed at the drop of a dime.

"He's in Alabama?" Sasha persisted.

I nodded.

"He's got no other family besides his parents who are in jail," she explained. "Someone in Alabama must've taken pity on him."

The new information about Crosby whirled around my head, answering so many questions I'd had about him. Explaining so many things.

"Isn't he so stinkin' hot?" Sasha said, interrupting my thoughts.

Everyone burst into laughter, never expecting something like that to come out of her mouth.

"All those tattoos. *Gah*," she continued. "You're so lucky he's at your school."

I thought back to the feel of those tattooed arms around me on the dance floor and the way his chest pressed to my back sent chills through my body. Then I remembered how that dance ended. "So, his parents are really in jail?"

Sasha nodded.

Knots of unease formed in my stomach as guilt crept into my chest.

While Aunt Pat continued discussing Crosby and his parents like she knew them, I grabbed my phone from beside me on my chair and checked the hockey schedule. The team didn't have a game until January twelfth. I pinched the bridge of my nose and squeezed my eyes shut. Was he alone on campus? Alone on the holiday? Alone until January twelfth?

That night, after everyone left, I lay in bed scrolling through news stories about Crosby's parents. It was as Aunt Pat had said. Millions of dollars embezzled. Millions of dollars owed. Pictures of Crosby's parents in the courtroom accompanied most of the articles. His mother was a beautiful woman. Her perfectly coiffed blonde hair showed sophistication, but her eyes showed regret and pain. His father was an older version of Crosby. Same dark hair. Same intense blue eyes. But his dad's eyes told stories of deceit—not regret for stealing from innocent people or for letting down his only son.

I wondered how Crosby felt about his parents now. Did he love the people who brought him into this world or despise the greedy people they'd become—the ones who destroyed his family and the life he'd been brought up in?

I moved on from the stories about his parents and searched social media. Crosby had no accounts. No social media presence at all. Had he been forced to shut down his accounts after everything happened or was he just not into stuff like that? I guess I didn't know him well enough to know the answer.

My search gave way to a miserable night of tossing and turning. I was unable to sleep as thoughts of Crosby alone on the holiday consumed my mind. He had no one, and regardless of our differences, that was not okay with me.

* * *

I awoke the day after Christmas, exhausted from not having slept for more than two hours. I stumbled out of bed and showered. Guilty thoughts plagued my mind. My last conversation with Crosby sat at the forefront of my brain, and my constant lack of tolerance for him turned my stomach. I was better than that.

After my shower, I dropped down onto a stool at the kitchen island where my mom cooked breakfast and my dad read the newspaper. "Morning."

My dad glanced over the top of his newspaper at me. "Morning."

My mom placed a glass of orange juice down in front of me. "Why are you already showered and dressed?"

I wrapped my hands around my glass but didn't drink it. "Well…"

My dad folded his newspaper in front of him, ready for whatever I planned to say.

"You've always taught me to never have regrets," I began.

"I feel like I might need to sit down for this," my mom said as she abandoned the food and sat down beside me.

I spent the next twenty minutes explaining what had happened on campus since the night I stumbled upon Crosby tied to the tree. My parents agreed—as I knew they would—that the only way to feel right about something unsettling was to do something about it.

CHAPTER THIRTEEN

Sabrina

I knew I was about to do something completely insane because I didn't call Finlay, *and* I didn't stop driving the entire six hours. I feared if I stopped, I would've talked myself out of it.

When I pulled onto campus with my gas tank teetering on empty, it was a ghost town. No one walked on the paths. No cars were parked in front of buildings or occupied the deserted lots. I pulled in front of the dorm behind mine and switched off my ignition.

What the hell was I doing?

I dropped my forehead onto the steering wheel and closed my eyes. What if he wasn't there? What if he had a girl in there? What if I was making the biggest mistake of my life?

It had been a long trip. I was tired and cranky. Maybe having Trish turn on me really did a number on my sanity. Maybe I wasn't thinking straight at all. I'd had six hours to consider my actions, but I'd drowned out my thoughts with loud music and junk food during my trip.

I guess I knew in my heart, it was the right thing to do. It was normal to help someone in need. Even if I did hate that person most of the time.

A loud bang on my window jarred me upright, sending my heart walloping. I turned slowly. Crosby stood outside on the sidewalk staring in at me. I wasn't ready to see him yet. I had no idea what I even planned to say.

Exhaling a deep breath, I pushed open the door. Crosby took a couple steps back as I stepped onto the sidewalk, stretching my legs for the first time in hours.

"What are you doing here?" he asked, a tinge of anger in his voice.

"What am *I* doing here?" I looked around the empty streets and sidewalks. "Care to tell me what you're doing on this deserted campus?"

"It's not deserted. Me and the exchange students are doing just fine."

I shook my head, wanting to laugh but feeling sorry for him at the same time. His parents were in jail. He had no one. It wasn't funny. It was unfortunate.

He crossed his arms, flashing those colorful tattoos right in my face. For the first time, I noticed a bright green four-leafed clover on his left inner forearm. Swirls of black wrapped around both arms and what looked like hockey pucks shaded in the bare areas connecting everything together. "You still haven't told me what you're doing here," he said.

Instead of meeting his eyes, I reached into my open car door and grabbed the handle on the paper bag in the passenger seat. I stepped back and extended it to him. "I brought leftovers."

His wide eyes looked about ready to burst from their sockets. "For me?"

"Don't sound so surprised."

"Surprised is definitely an understatement," he said.

"Just thought you might like them."

"How'd you know I'd be here?"

I shrugged, my guilty eyes averting his and latching onto a lone bird soaring through the overcast sky.

"So, you know my shit?"

I glanced back to him. "Just what the news said."

He scoffed as he shook his head. "I'm surprised it took this long." He spun away from me and headed toward his building.

The fact that he'd left me standing alone on a deserted sidewalk with the bag of leftovers in my hand was not lost on me. As I glanced around the empty campus, anger raged inside me. Why had I shown up? Why had I gone out of my way for this jerk? We weren't even friends. We were nothing to each other.

"Aren't you coming?" he called as he reached the front door of his building.

I buried my free hand in my hip and stared across the space between us. "Why should I?"

He turned slowly and gazed at me. "How far did you drive?"

"Six hours."

He said nothing, just nodded as if it made perfect sense I'd drive all that way for him. "Come on. I don't want to eat alone."

Did I stand my ground and head back home? Six hours was a long way to drive back angry. Besides, I needed to pee.

I released a breath and walked to the door. His eyes followed me as he held the door open for me. I brushed by him, stepping inside the silent foyer. It was then, as our shoes echoed up the stairs, I realized how very alone we actually were.

Crosby

I pushed open the door to my room, hoping it wasn't too much of a disaster. Sabrina had stopped by the restroom, so I hurried over to my desk and shoved some things in drawers. Then, I moved to my unmade bed and tugged up the blue comforter.

"Nice place," she said, walking inside with the bag of food she'd brought me from six fucking hours away. I still couldn't wrap my head around it. This girl who barely knew me—this girl I'd repeatedly been a dick to, drove six hours from another state to make sure I wasn't alone the day after Christmas.

Go fucking figure.

"You can put that down over there." I pointed toward my desk.

She placed what I assumed to be a monster meal down and glanced around my empty room. The walls were bare and my hockey sticks and equipment bag stood in the corner.

I gestured toward my bed. "Feel free to sit."

She lifted her brows presumptuously.

"I'll be a gentleman," I assured her with a small grin.

"You sure? I took you for someone who couldn't control it."

I tossed back my head and laughed. "You're pretty sure of yourself, aren't you?"

"Look at me," she teased, glancing purposefully down at her torn jeans and hoodie.

"Oh, and you're funny."

She lifted a shoulder as she sat down on the edge of my bed. "Don't forget smart and talented."

I laughed again, wishing I could hug her for being what I needed in that moment. But knowing what I knew of her, she probably would've kneed me in the balls. "I'm gonna have to agree on both accounts."

She cocked her head. "How do you know I'm smart?"

I walked over to the bag of food she'd brought and reached inside, pulling out a clear plastic container filled with slices of ham.

"Well, you brought me ham and not turkey."

"You don't like turkey?"

"Nope. See? Smart." I pulled out another container filled with roasted potatoes.

"So, how do you know I'm talented?" she asked with amusement coloring her tone.

I glanced over my shoulder at her sitting on my bed. So many inappropriate words sat at the tip of my tongue as my eyes moved slowly over her curves. Her chest. Her pretty face.

"I'm waiting," she said, clearly knowing where my thoughts had ventured to.

"I'm editing my thoughts."

The sweet sound of her laughter filled my room.

I smiled and, for the first time in a long fucking time, I wasn't faking it. It had been over a year since I'd heard genuine laughter that had the ability to relax me and thaw my hardened heart. It sucked it came from a girl who hated me ninety-nine percent of the time.

Sabrina stood and closed the distance between us. I stilled, not wanting to do anything to make her feel uncomfortable in such close quarters. She brushed by me, moving to the bag and reaching inside. "I'm starving," she said, pulling out the remaining containers, plastic dishes, and silverware.

Once she'd opened the containers, a mixture of delicious smells filled my room.

We piled our dishes with ham, beef tenderloin, asparagus, rice, potatoes, and two types of pie. Sabrina sat back down on my bed while I sat backward on my desk chair, enjoying a quiet meal.

Sabrina seemed comfortable in my space. What was I saying? The girl exuded confidence and was comfortable in her own skin. It was clear in the way she entered a room. In the way she knew eyes were on her but she let them stare. In the way her clothes hugged her body in all the right places. Some girls used their looks to get them what they wanted. She didn't. She knew she was hot, but relied on her intelligence and sass to get her what she wanted.

"Your mom made all of this?" I asked with a mouthful.

She nodded. "I helped with the pies."

"Everything's delicious."

"Would've been a shame to let it all go to waste. My parents don't eat leftovers, and I couldn't eat it all myself."

"No siblings?"

She shook her head. "You either?"

"Nope." I finished off a slice of pie. "Did you have a nice Christmas?"

"Yeah."

I could tell by her clipped response she didn't want to make me feel bad for having a shitty one. "You don't have to do that."

Her eyes flashed up from her mostly empty dish. "What?"

"Downplay the holiday. Just because mine sucked didn't mean yours had to."

"That's not what I was doing."

"Regardless. You showed up here with food for an asshole like me. In my book, you can talk about whatever the hell you want to and I'll listen. Unless you're into reality TV, then I'm out."

She smiled, a comeback sitting at the ready. But instead, she lifted her fork to her mouth and ate another bite of food.

"So, tell me what Santa brought you."

She shrugged. "Just some clothes and a new phone."

"That's cool."

She continued eating.

Before I allowed an uncomfortable silence to creep its way in, I reached for my phone and queued up some holiday music. A Christmas song filled the silence.

Sabrina smiled. "Didn't take you for the Christmas music type of guy."

"Oh no?"

She shook her head. "Heavy metal maybe."

I snickered. "Because of all the anger I've got bottled up inside?"

She stared at me, her eyes filled with wonder. "Do you?"

"Do I what?"

"Have anger bottled up inside?"

I shrugged. "It's pretty hard not to when your parents are in jail, your friends deserted you, and your broke ass can barely afford a phone. It's just a matter of time before it gets shut off."

The sympathy in her eyes was difficult to miss. "I'm sorry."

"You didn't steal money from innocent people. You've got nothing to be sorry about."

"I meant I'm sorry this happened. I'm sorry they didn't think about where it might leave you."

I grabbed a napkin off the desk and wiped it across my mouth. "If I've learned anything from what happened, it's money isn't the root of all evil. Greed is. My grandparents left my dad very well off. He didn't need to embezzle money. But he did. And I hate him for it."

"It must be hard hating someone you're supposed to love."

I crumbled up my napkin and tossed it into the small trash can in the corner. "It sucks."

"You didn't mention your mom."

"She was an unknowing accomplice. Signing paperwork she didn't read and allowing my father to put her name on everything business-related."

Sabrina nodded, and though she had no idea what it was like to be me, I believed she understood my pain.

We finished off our meals and Sabrina stood, grabbing our empty dishes and tossing them into the now empty bag.

Worry suddenly twisted my gut. Did she plan to head back home now that we'd eaten? Had she done her good deed for the year? Was she now off to bestow pity on someone else? Anger crept in. The type I couldn't control. The type that overtook my thoughts and shook my bones.

"So, what should we do now?" she asked.

Her words stilled my anger. "You're not leaving?"

Her mouth parted slightly. "Oh…I just thought…"

Oh, fuck. "No, I meant I didn't think you'd want to hang around here."

"No, that's fine." She scrambled around trying to secure the covers on the food containers. "My dorm's one of them they close over break, so I can head home."

I jumped to my feet and stepped up behind her, reaching around and stopping her hands from frantically stuffing empty containers into the bag. She stiffened as my hands circled her tiny wrists and my chest pressed to her back. Her peach scent invaded my senses as it had that night on the dance floor. We stood like that for a long moment, both breathing unsteadily. "I want you to stay."

She said nothing.

"No one has ever done something this nice for me before."

She remained silent.

"I want you here with me." I dropped my hands as she twisted to face me.

We were mere inches from each other. She stared into my eyes and, for the first time, it was as if she saw someone she didn't hate. She looked at me like she could see all the way down to the depths of who I was. I almost asked what she discovered, since so many pieces of me had been broken over the last year. "Am I getting Crosby or Mr. Hockey?"

I scoffed, though having her lips so close to mine did weird things to my train of thought. "Which would you prefer?"

Her mouth twisted as she deliberated. "Mr. Hockey's arrogance is unparalleled."

I stifled a snicker given the honesty in her tone.

"But Crosby is easier to talk to."

"Then Crosby it is."

"It's that easy?"

"Yup. Now come on. I wanna take you somewhere."

Her brows shot up. "Will you be bringing rope?"

I laughed. "No. I wanna take you to the rink."

"You planning to show off?"

Realizing I was still so close to her, I stepped back. "Maybe."

She laughed and I was beginning to like her laugh more than I had the right to. "Well, I can't skate, so I'll hang in the seats and watch."

"You can't skate?"

"I'm from Florida. Not much ice there."

"Same in Texas. But we have these things called ice rinks."

She shoved my arm, which made me laugh harder. "Oh, so you're funny?"

"Don't forget smart and talented—just like you," I said.

She shook her head and walked to my door. "Come on. Before I start hating you again."

"You never hated me."

Her laughter as she walked out the door told me she definitely had.

Sabrina

While Crosby took off for the locker room to grab something, I walked to the opening in the rink wall and tested the ice with the tip of my sneaker. The surface was smoother than I imagined and too slippery for me to feel comfortable standing on it.

"You coming?" Crosby said as he skated toward me from the opposite end of the dark rink.

The last time Crosby skated toward me in that rink, I felt nothing but disdain for him. This time, as he made his way toward me in jeans and a T-shirt, I smiled. Being there with him made absolutely no sense at all. Me *liking* being there with him made even less sense.

He held up a pair of hockey skates. "Put these on."

"You're kidding?"

"Scared?"

I snatched the skates from his hand. "Why don't you show me what you've got while I put these on."

His lips slipped into a cocky smirk as I sat down in the nearest seat. "You sure you can handle it?"

I pulled off my sneakers and slipped my feet into the hockey skates. "I'm not easily impressed."

"Sounds like a challenge."

I shrugged as I proceeded to lace up the skates.

Crosby turned away from me and zigzagged down the length of the ice faster than I'd ever seen someone skate in person. I thought he'd crash into the far wall, but he swerved quickly and skated toward me—backward.

Damn show off.

I stood unsteadily on my skates and held onto the seat in front of me, slowly making my way to the opening in the rink.

When he reached me, he spun, scraping the ice with his blades and spraying frost all over my legs.

I suppressed a grin. "Not impressed."

His brows shot up. "Oh no?"

I shook my head.

"What's it gonna take?"

I lifted my chin at the ice. "More than that."

He glided forward until he stopped in front of me in the open doorway. "Be careful what you ask for."

It happened before I saw it coming. He grabbed me and tossed me over his shoulder, taking off and circling the ice at top speed with me hanging upside down and screaming like a maniac. "Put me down!"

His deep laughter filled the arena, echoing off the empty seats.

"I'm serious!" I shrieked as I held on to his hips for dear life.

My pleas didn't faze him. He moved faster and in ways that would surely send me flying off his shoulder if he fell. But he didn't. His movements were smooth, his turns effortless. If I wasn't so scared of landing face-first into the ice, I might've enjoyed the ride more. "You impressed yet?" he asked.

"Yes!" I screeched.

"I don't believe you." He spun, whipping me around and skating backward.

I closed my eyes and buried my face in his back. "I'm impressed!"

His shoulders shook with laughter as he slowed to a stop at the side of the ice. He guided me over his shoulder and down his front until he placed me on my skates.

I glared into his light eyes as I held the sides of his arms for support. I wanted to be pissed at him for scaring the hell out of me, but his flushed cheeks, deep breaths, and grin softened my anger.

Damn him.

"That was fun," Crosby said.

My feet slipped on the ice beneath me, so I inched my way over to the nearby wall, releasing my hold on Crosby and grasping onto it with a death-grip. "I'm glad you thought so."

He laughed. "Come on. You have to admit it's fun being out here. The crispness of the air. The breeze in your face. The speed of the ice."

"If my butt wasn't pointing north the whole time, I might've appreciated it a little bit more."

He ticked his head toward the center of the ice. "Come on then."

My eyes dropped down to my skates.

He held out his hand. "I've got you."

I stared at his outstretched hand, noticing the interesting way his tattoos cut off at his wrist. Not being one to show fear, I grabbed hold of his hand. He linked his finger with mine. His grip was strong and warm, something I hadn't realized I needed in the cold arena.

He eased me off the wall and basically walked on his skates so I could slip my way around the ice. "See you're doing it."

"Barely."

We moved slowly around the perimeter of the ice with him pulling me along as I kept my skates as steady as I could.

As we approached the first turn, he squeezed my hand. I figured he was keeping me from falling, but then he spoke softly. "Thanks."

I gave him a sidelong glance as I struggled not to fall on my butt. "For what?"

"Showing up."

I couldn't be sure if I wanted to smile at the vulnerability he was displaying or cry for the boy inside him who'd lost everything. "I have a habit of showing up, don't I?"

He snickered. "I guess you do."

"Well, if you stopped giving me reasons to, I wouldn't have to." I bumped him with my hip which probably wasn't the best idea since I could barely stay upright on my own.

"Now where would the fun in that be?"

I smiled as I leaned into his arm for support as we slowly made it through the first full corner. "So, do you miss Texas?"

"Yup."

"That was fast. You hate it that much here?"

"Yup."

"Oh, thanks," I said, feigning insult.

"No, I just meant—"

I laughed. "I know what you meant. I was teasing you."

Once we'd circled the ice one time, I wondered if he'd stop at the open doorway. He didn't. We proceeded around again. This time I felt more comfortable, though a triple axel would not be in my future. "Why'd you choose hockey? You suck at football or something?"

He choked on a laugh. "Did you seriously just say that?"

"I did."

A flicker of amusement lit his eyes. "No, I didn't suck at football. I chose hockey for the fights."

I laughed. "Does every hockey player say that?"

"Probably." Unexpectedly, he stopped and moved in front of me, grabbing my other hand so he held both. I couldn't peel my eyes away from his, wondering what he had planned. "Let's get you moving a little faster."

"That sounds like a terrible idea."

While facing me, he skated backward and pulled me forward. "Don't worry. I've got you if you fall."

I didn't doubt it. And that scared the hell out of me.

We'd nearly made it around the ice another full time when the front of my skate caught a bump in the ice and sent me toppling forward. Crosby didn't expect me to crash into his chest because his legs shot out in unnatural directions. He fought to remain upright, but he fell backward with me clutched to his chest.

"Ohmigod," I squealed as I closed my eyes and landed with a thud on top of him.

A long silence passed. I didn't open my eyes for fear of Crosby's reaction. Would Mr. Hockey rear his ugly head?

My eyes cracked open.

Crosby dropped his head back on the ice and laughter burst out of him. The sound echoed around the empty rink.

"What's so funny? Are you hurt?"

He lifted his head to look at me. "You weigh a hundred pounds. I'm fine."

Instinctively, my hands shot out and my fingers slipped through the back of his hair, feeling for a bump. "Did you hit your head?"

"I told you I'm fine. If you don't stop fussing over me, I might think you actually like me."

I snorted. "It's gonna take more than fancy skating to get me to like you."

He gazed into my eyes with a small grin on his face but said nothing.

"What?"

He shook his head, though his eyes riveted between mine for another long moment. "Stay."

My brows shot up. "What?"

"Don't go home. Stay here with me."

A weird sensation swirled in my belly. What was he asking? What did he think was going on between us? "Why?"

"Because you're the closest thing I've got to a friend these days, and I really don't want you to leave."

The desperation of his words, mixed with the honesty in his gaze, pricked my eyes with tears. I didn't cry easily, but in that moment, with him beneath me awaiting my response, I realized he truly had no one but me.

But how long did he want me to stay? For the night? For the week? Until school began again? I guess it didn't matter. I didn't have anything going on back home. And no one but my parents would miss me, and they were leaving for a two-week cruise in mid-January anyway. "Okay."

His smile nearly erased every bad thought I'd ever had about him. How was this the same guy I'd met in November?

By the time we returned to his room, the sun had set and his room was pitch black. He flipped on the light. And suddenly the space was too small. Too silent. Too stifling.

What had I agreed to?

"You wanna watch a movie?" Crosby asked, gesturing toward his bed.

"A movie?"

"Yeah. What'd you think I was gonna do? Get you back here and try to get you naked?"

"Kinda."

He snickered. "Well, you're here. Does that mean I misread things?" He climbed onto the bed and crossed his arms behind his head with his legs outstretched in front of him. "We can totally forget the movie."

I rolled my eyes.

Crosby laughed as he sat up, pushing himself back so he leaned against the wall. "Come on," he said, grabbing his tablet from his nightstand and tapping away at the screen.

I walked over and sat, kicking off my shoes before leaning beside him and stretching out my legs.

He called up a couple movies. I pointed to the recent blockbuster I hadn't seen. He looked to me. "Seriously?"

"I love action movies. *And*, I wouldn't want you to fall asleep watching a chick flick."

He bumped me with his shoulder. "You're all right, you know that?"

"Yup," I said, as he selected the movie. "It's about time you figured it out."

He smiled as the opening credits appeared on the screen.

We watched the movie in comfortable silence. It gave me time to think. Since arriving back on campus, I hadn't had time to consider what I'd done by showing up—or even how I really felt about Crosby now that I'd gotten to know him a little better. He'd entered my life unexpectedly and turned it upside down at times, but he was different than I imagined. Funnier. Thoughtful. Calmer.

Crosby pulled in a deep breath beside me and released it slowly. I wondered what he was thinking. Was he thinking about me the way I was thinking about him? Or was he just focused on the movie like I should've been?

One thing I was beginning to understand was the reason for his split personalities. He didn't know who to trust. His parents screwed him over and then the guys on the team made his transition to our school hell. It made sense that he wouldn't freely open himself up to people he just met. I guess with him you had to earn it. Was that what was happening between us? Had he been gauging whether or not he could trust me? *Was* he starting to trust me?

I thought back to the confident way he moved on the ice while showing off for me earlier. The gentle way he held onto me and guided me around the ice. The way he protected me with his body when I oh-so-gracefully knocked us down. Every girl wanted to be treated like she was someone special. And as crazy as it was to admit, being alone with Crosby on the ice made me feel that way.

Beside me, Crosby lifted his hand to his chin, moving his fingers lightly over the stubble dusting his jawline. His arm brushed mine as he did and I tensed. It had been some time since I'd been alone on a bed in a dark room with a guy. And most of the time, even if we'd begun our night watching a movie, we didn't finish the movie.

My imagination began to run wild. Was Crosby moving his hand a calculated effort to move closer? Was he planning to reach over and try to touch me? Try to grab my hand? Try to…something? We were all alone. No one would interrupt. No one would stop us.

But a minute later, he dropped his hand and was engrossed in the movie.

Inside, I cringed at the inaccuracy of my thoughts.

But now that my traitorous mind had begun to wander, I was becoming more and more aware of Crosby's presence. His steady breathing beside me. His woodsy fresh scent filling the air. His strong body pressed into my side.

It had been over a year since I'd been with a guy. Was I just horny? Did the darkness automatically mean hooking up for me?

My heartbeat began to quicken, and I felt it thumping everywhere.

Shit.

Twenty-four hours ago, I hated Crosby. Why all of a sudden was my body so attuned to his?

He shifted his butt over an inch or two. I held my breath. Was this the moment he'd make a move?

Nope. He was just getting more comfortable.

Frustration crept into my bones. Was I actually disappointed he hadn't tried anything? Was he not attracted to me? Was I not his type?

After a few more car chases and explosions on the screen, the movie ended. I remained silent and still, a ball of confused nerves.

Crosby turned to look at me. Could he tell where my thoughts had been? Had he felt my heartbeat racing? Had he felt me tense up every time he moved his body?

"You can take the bed," he said, breaking the silence and reining in my thoughts.

"I'm not taking your bed," I said, internally berating myself for jumping to conclusions. "It's your room."

"And you're my guest." He rolled over, careful not to touch me as he hopped over me and stood up. "Where are your keys?"

"I left them on your desk."

He switched on a small desk light and found my keys, scooping them up and heading to the door.

"What are you doing?"

"Grabbing your things."

I watched as he turned and left the room, still taken aback by this thoughtful side of him. If I'd met this version of Crosby that night at the tree, would things have turned out differently between us? Or were things unraveling just as they were supposed to?

"Thanks," I said when Crosby returned a couple minutes later with my suitcase. "I so need to brush my teeth."

He laughed as he placed my suitcase down in front of me.

I rummaged through it, grabbing my toiletries bag and some cute pajamas. Crosby grabbed his own toothbrush and toothpaste from his drawer, and we left his room together, parting ways at our respective bathrooms.

I brushed my teeth and dressed in the women's room, giving myself time to calm myself and control the thoughts I'd been having.

When I returned to his room a little while later, he was already back, pulling a spare pillow and blanket from the top of his closet and placing them on the floor.

"You sure you don't want the bed?" I asked.

"I'm sure."

I stuffed my clothes and toiletries back into my suitcase, trying to ignore the fact that he was pulling off his shirt and jeans so that he was only wearing his boxers. The sight of him standing there, so comfortably shirtless in front me, was so damn hot my breath hitched in my throat.

I sat down on his bed, trying to steady my heartbeat. His colorful tattoos overwhelmed my eyes. There were so many of them. "Tell me about your tattoos."

He smirked as he leaned against his chair, glancing down at the sleeves of ink on his arms. "What do you wanna know?"

"Why so many?"

He met my gaze. "Why not?"

Okay. Stupid question. "Which was your first?"

He twisted his right arm to show the inside of his forearm. Crisscrossed hockey sticks.

"Typical."

He laughed. "What'd you expect? A heart with a girl's name in the center?"

"Maybe."

He rotated his arm, pointing out all the others. From skulls to tribal bands, everything was connected. His left arm looked similar. More hockey symbols, wings, a number representing the date of his first goal, and a quote about teammates.

"Did you all get that one?"

He balked. "Yeah."

"You regret it now?"

"Friends stick by you. Mine didn't." He shrugged it off but I could see it bothered him in the way his eyes drifted away.

I pointed to the bare spot on the inside of his left bicep. "Run out of ideas?"

He shook his head. "Nah. All my tattoos have been for me. I left that spot for whoever I marry. I figure anyone tough enough to deal with me, deserves a prime spot."

My bottom lip jutted out, both surprised and impressed he'd thought ahead. "You know, that's kind of romantic. You don't want anyone thinking you've gone soft, do you?"

He laughed as he switched off the light and sat on the blanket on the floor. "I'm not all angry, you know?"

I nodded, though in the darkness I couldn't be sure he saw me. "I'm starting to see that."

I faintly saw him lay down on his back and cross his arms behind his head. I crawled under the sheets on his bed and turned on my side so I could face him.

A long silence passed between us.

"Sorry we got off on the wrong foot," he said.

"Sorry I left you tied to a tree."

"Are you?"

I laughed. "Not really. You deserved it."

I could hear the smile in his voice. "Good night, Sabrina."

"Good night, Crosby."

But it wasn't a good night. Not even close. I was up most of it listening to the low purr of Crosby's breathing. It was all I could focus on. The guy was jacked. And those tattoos—now that I'd seen them up close and knew what they meant to him—made him even hotter. And don't get me started on his naked body. I'd somehow been able to put that image out of my head, but now that we were alone in the darkness, and it's all I could think about.

My body tingled with need. I'd never been one who couldn't control my urges. Control my thoughts from going to dirty places. Control the throbbing between my thighs.

Ugh.

I rolled onto my stomach and buried my face in the pillow. The damn thing had Crosby's scent all over it.

Fuuuuuck.

CHAPTER FOURTEEN

Sabrina

The sound of Crosby's door closing softly jarred me awake in the morning. Feeling groggy and exhausted, my eyes cracked open. Sunlight filtered into the room. Crosby wasn't there, but I could hear the soft rasp of his voice in the hallway.

"I'm fine," he said. "How are you doing?" Since there was no other voice, it was clear he was on the phone. "Yeah...Appeal it…That sounds like a good idea." Nothing in his voice said he believed what he said. "I'll try. You know I don't have a car anymore. I'd have to take the bus again…Uh huh…Thanks for calling. Talk to you tomorrow." There was a long silence. I wondered if he was listening to whichever parent was on the other end or if he'd disconnected the call and needed time to regroup.

A short while later, the door handle twisted. Crosby stepped inside the room and closed the door behind him.

"You okay?" I asked.

He swung around. "Sorry. I didn't mean to wake you."

I sat up, pulling an elastic from my wrist and tying my hair into a top-knot. "You didn't."

"Oh, good." He hurried to his closet and grabbed a towel. Then he moved just as quickly to his dresser, grabbed a pair of boxers, and walked to the door. "I'm gonna take a shower."

"Oh. Okay," I said, trying to figure out why he suddenly seemed so eager to get away from me. Was he regretting asking me to stay?

He pulled open the door.

"Wait."

He twisted toward me.

"You sure you're okay?"

He stared across the room at me, his eyes saying what his answer didn't. "Yeah."

When he walked back into his room twenty minutes later with soaked hair wearing only his boxers, I focused solely on his eyes. And not the droplets of water on his face. Or the ridges defining the muscles in his chest. Or the tattoos wrapped around his arms.

"Is it safe for me out there?" I flicked my eyes toward the door.

He nodded. "No one else is on the floor. But I'll leave my door open so I can hear if anyone shows up." He walked to his closet and grabbed a towel. "Here." He tossed it to me.

I caught it and grabbed the clothes and shower supplies I had waiting beside me. Clutching them to my chest, I walked to the door, making sure not to brush into any part of him as I stepped into the hallway. If my thoughts the previous night were any indication, the sight of him all wet from a shower was setting off major warning signs. "Be back in a few."

He nodded, quickly turning away from me.

I hurried into the girls' shower room. The six-stalled room was empty and silent. Finally, I could breathe. I could think straight. I switched on the water. The spray drowned out the silence, but in no way stopped the inappropriate thoughts from running through my brain.

I needed to leave. I needed to head home. If I stayed, whatever happened between us had disaster written all over it. The water continued to cascade over my body, washing Crosby's scent off me with each passing minute.

As the minutes ticked on, my mind taunted me with visions I wanted to suppress. Me on top of him at the rink. His strong body beneath mine. His arms wrapped tightly around me. His raspy laughter. I shivered at the thoughts. Or maybe it was the water turning colder since I'd been hiding in the shower for so long.

Eventually, I switched off the knob and reached for the towel hanging outside my stall, wrapping it around me as I stepped out. It smelled like Crosby. That fresh woodsy scent—the one I now realized was all his—enveloped me. I closed my eyes and breathed it in. In such a short time, it had become so familiar and comfortable.

Shit, shit, shit.

I needed to refocus.

I dragged my fingers through my wet hair, eliminating the knots as I walked to the changing area where I'd left my clothes.

A knock on the door stilled me.

"Sabrina?" Crosby called through the door.

"Yeah."

"You okay? You've been gone a while."

The concern in his voice caused unwanted ripples to swell in my belly. "Fine," I called, before listening for his footsteps to walk away. They didn't.

"Can I come in?" The gruffness in his voice, mixed with his question, sent heat coursing through my body.

"Ummm. Okay."

The door opened slowly until Crosby stood in the doorway looking exactly as he had when he returned from his shower. Why hadn't he gotten dressed? Why was he there? His eyes moved over my towel-covered body, his appraisal slow and purposeful as the door closed behind him. We were alone. *Very* alone.

I swallowed hard. "Everything okay?"

The silence was deafening as he took two steps closer to me. "How long are we gonna do this?"

"Do what?" I asked, though my heartbeat speeding in my chest told me I already knew the answer.

He took another step. Then another. Until he stood in front of me. He was a head taller, so I lifted my head back to meet his gaze. "I am trying so hard to be good."

A cacophony of thoughts rushed through my head, none making much sense.

Dammit.

Crosby reached up and brushed his thumb over my cheek, leaving a numbness in its wake. "But all I can smell in my room is you," he said, his voice hushed.

My pulse hastened.

"All I can think about in my bed is you."

I blinked, swallowing down hard.

He stepped forward, causing me to step back into the cool tiled wall behind me. I sucked in a deep breath as he caged me in with his hands on the wall. "And all I want to do is kiss you."

My eyes dropped to his lips. God, they were glistening and perfect.

"And the way you're looking at my mouth right now tells me I'm not the only one feeling this way."

My eyes jumped to his. They were zoned in on mine and dilated. *Oh, man.* My breathing became labored. Would kissing him ease my confusion? Would scratching that itch help me to hate him again or would I get myself in deeper?

His hands cupped my cheeks, strong and possessive. He stared into my eyes, his riveting between them. He was giving me time to stop him. Time to consider what his next move would inevitably be. I pulled in another deep breath and that's all the assurance he needed. His lips crashed down on mine. They were fierce and determined, and hot as holy hell. My lips parted. His tongue plunged inside my mouth, tangling with mine in desperate pursuit. We both fought for control. Fought against what we initially thought about each other. And truth be told, it made the kiss so much hotter. All the pent up sexual tension he and I had been dancing around had finally come to a head. An explosive head.

Crosby's hands slipped to the back of my head, cradling it from the hard tiles as his bare chest pressed to mine, pinning me with nowhere to go. He shifted his hips. His erection pressed through his boxers and into my towel, the only real barrier between us. The ache between my thighs came hard and fast, throbbing like a ticking time bomb. Craving the feel of him, I wrapped my arms around his neck, arching into him as his mouth continued to move ferociously with mine. Though it was impossible to get any closer, his hands slipped down my back, pulling me against his chest. His hands continued down until they reached the bottom of my towel. I stilled. So did his hands.

He pulled back enough to see my eyes. We were both breathing heavy. Both turned on beyond reason. "I don't wanna screw this up," he said. "I need you to tell me if this is going too fast."

My body was a live wire ready to ignite if he didn't stop talking and ease my ache. No way did I want him getting all self-righteous now. My hands pulled him toward me and my lips captured his. The low contented hum in the back of his throat urged me on. But Crosby was in no way passive. He kissed me back, his hands slipping beneath my towel and drifting over my bare ass as his mouth moved with mine. "I want you," he murmured against my lips.

"I'm right here."

I squeaked as he lifted me off my feet and stormed out of the shower room. I laughed at the determination in his eyes as he walked us down the deserted hallway and through his open door, slamming it closed behind us. Once inside it was a whole different story. No one would interrupt us there. This could go as far as I let it.

He lowered me onto his bed, following me down slowly. With his forearms on the pillow beside my head, his strong body pressed me into the mattress and his mouth returned to mine. His body moved over me. Through the towel, his erection hit my clit, sending my eyes rolling into the back of my head. He kept at it, torturing me with the feel of him. He was looking for the okay. Looking for something that told him I was okay with what was happening.

I slipped my arms around his back. The ridges were taut and the skin smooth beneath my touch. I continued down to the dip above his ass, reaching the band on his boxers. I slipped my fingertips underneath. He pulled away from my lips and dropped his mouth to my neck, assaulting my skin with open-mouthed kisses that were focused. Deep. Intoxicating. My head drifted to the side as my hands continued down, drifting over his ass and around his muscular hips.

He growled into my neck. "Make sure you know what you're doing."

"You think I don't know what I'm doing?" I challenged, my hand moving to the front and grabbing hold of the hard length between us.

"*Fuuuuuck*," he hissed.

My hand tightened, moving up and down in a smooth rhythmic motion. "You should know I love a challenge."

His laugh rumbled deep, vibrating against my neck before his lips moved back to mine. This kiss was fierce, his tongue diving deeper, stroking inside my mouth and entwining with mine. His hand descended, sliding into the opening of my towel. His fingers found the dampness between my thighs.

Holy mother of all things glory.

He spread my folds and his fingers drifted gently over the swollen skin.

My head fell back, pushing into the pillow as my hand continued moving over him. "Oh, God.

Two of his fingers pushed inside me. My back arched off the bed. But he didn't stop there. His thumb found my clit and circled it. Around and around. A groan reverberated deep in my chest as I squirmed beneath him, releasing my grasp on his erection. He pressed his thumb harder, moving up and down. The tingles in my body coiled in that spot. He seemed to know because his fingers began pumping in and out of me as his thumb moved around in circles again, this time slowly. Oh so slowly. He taunted me, circling then gliding over it. Then circling some more.

The tingles built again, this time a flood of euphoria sat ready to unleash. My eyes pinched tight as my body went off like a cork, ripples firing out to all parts of my body. I struggled to catch my breath as his relentless fingers kept at it, milking every last bit of pleasure from me. I couldn't take the torture. I writhed beneath him, trying unsuccessfully to buck him off my quaking body.

He eventually relented, removing his fingers and letting me enjoy the aftershocks rippling through me. "God, I wish you could see your face right now."

My eyes fluttered open. "Why?"

"Because you look so damn beautiful."

I scoffed. "Underneath you?"

He shook his head, embarrassment flashing in his eyes. "I can be a real asshole sometimes."

"After what you've been through, it's to be expected. But, so you know, not everyone will let you down."

He flashed a cocky smirk. "That's what I'm hoping if you wrap that little hand of yours around my dick again."

"*Annnnd* Mr. Hockey's back."

He laughed and I really liked the raspy sound of it, especially since I was the one to bring it out of him. But as quickly as it happened, it disappeared. "Why are you giving me a second chance?"

"More like a fifth chance."

He snickered.

I stared up into his blue eyes. They were so pretty and clear up close. So different than the angry ones I'd seen on more than one occasion. "Because I'm running out of reasons not to," I said.

Relief spread over his features as he leaned down and pressed his lips to mine. "Then I'd love to see what your hand and me have in common."

"As you wish, Mr. Hockey."

"You warming up to Mr. Hockey?"

"Only when he's talking dirty behind closed doors."

"I got you, girl," he assured me before rolling onto his back and taking me with him. My hand worked its magic until he was as breathless and sated as me. And then we slept, taking a much-needed afternoon nap together.

CHAPTER FIFTEEN

Crosby

Holy hell.

It had been some time since I'd had a gorgeous girl draped over me. And this one wore nothing but a towel. A towel I would've given anything to rip off her. But I was taking it slow. I would've been an idiot not to. We were essentially alone on a massive campus with nothing to pass the time but each other.

Sabrina's breath whooshed in and out of her lips softly, a quiet purr accompanying her sleep. She had this tough exterior, but asleep in my arms she was so vulnerable. But I would've been lying if I said watching that movie with her body pressed to my side hadn't been pure torture. I couldn't focus on the damn movie. I couldn't focus on anything but Sabrina in my room. On my bed. In every one of my thoughts.

I knew it had been a risk to pursue her in the shower room, but I needed to know if I was the only one feeling the sexual tension that had—in hindsight—been building between us for the past two months.

My body felt languid and, even with her partly naked body pressed against mine, I felt satisfied.

I thought back to the way her body reacted to my touch. Her sounds when she came. I could've listened to her groans and ragged breathing all night long. I thought back to her words. Thought back to her assurance that not everyone would let me down. Had I purposely kept people away? Is that what I'd been doing? Had the last year taught me not to trust anyone?

Sabrina stirred.

I wasn't ready for her to wake up yet. I liked watching her sleep. Liked feeling her on me. Liked having her there. She added light to the otherwise bleak existence I'd been living.

"Crosby," she whispered.

"Yeah?"

"I'm glad I came."

"So am I," I said, ecstatic to hear those words. "Nothing like leaving a girl unsatisfied."

She chuckled into my chest. "You know what I meant."

"Yeah."

"Will you tell me something?"

"I'm not a virgin?" I said.

She laughed. "You're so stupid."

I grinned and tightened my arms around her.

"Why do you let your teammates hurt you with no recourse?" she whispered.

My body tensed.

In the past when she questioned me about my teammates, it pissed me off. No one understood the anger and embarrassment their pranks elicited in me. I knew I looked like a pussy taking their shit. And I hated it. But now I realized, not only could Sabrina sense there was more to it, she actually cared. And that changed everything.

"If I suck it up, I'll enter the draft after the season and be done with it all. If I make waves, it could ruin my chances. Believe me, I wanna kick the shit outta everyone involved, but it'll only hurt me in the long run."

"I'm sorry."

"I can handle it."

She was silent again for a long time.

My fingertips drifted over her back, tracing small circles over the soft skin above the towel.

"There's gotta be a way to get even," she said.

"Oh, believe me. I've thought about it."

"We could hire someone."

"Hire someone?"

"Yeah. Haven't you seen those crime shows about people hiring hit men on the Internet?"

"I don't want to kill them."

She laughed. "No, not kill them. Hire someone to prank them or something. Oh my God. Did you really think I wanted you to put a hit out on the hockey team?"

"Kinda."

She snorted and it was so damn adorable.

"Thanks for trying to help. But it's gonna be okay."

Another long silence passed. I wondered if she was trying to decide if that was a lie or if she was just brainstorming more ways to bring down the hockey team. I liked that about her. She was determined and sassy and put up with no nonsense—not even mine.

"Are you planning to visit your parents?" she asked.

My body tensed at the mention of my parents. "Huh?"

"I heard you on the phone." She lifted her head and buried her chin in my chest. "Do you wanna see them?"

I shrugged. "Maybe my mom."

"Not your dad?"

I shook my head.

"I'm just gonna say this and you can do with it what you want. But bottling stuff inside eventually becomes too much. And as much as you're unhappy with your dad right now, you might feel better if you said whatever it is you really want to say to him. You know. Get it off your chest."

I hadn't thought of that. When I visited my mom, the sole purpose of my visit was to lift her spirits. No one said I had to do the same for my father. I could go in there and let him know how angry I was at him for destroying our family.

"I can drive you," Sabrina said.

My brows shot up. "To Texas?"

She nodded.

"It's eight hours away."

"I've got nowhere to be."

"There are a lot of places I'd like to take you. Prison's not one them."

She laughed. "We have time."

"Fuck." I jolted up, taking Sabrina with me. "What time is it?"

"What?"

I reached for my phone on my nightstand. Six o'clock. "I start my new job tonight."

"You've got a job?"

I'd been so caught up in Sabrina showing up that I'd forgotten my shift began at seven. "Yeah. Working security at the psych building." I rolled out from under her and raced to my dresser. "I need cash. I wouldn't be able to take you out if I didn't have any, would I?"

She rolled onto her side and propped herself up on her elbow. "You planning on taking me out?"

I stared down at her towel-clad body sprawled out on my bed, eating up her good looks. "Is that a trick question?"

She shook her head.

"Well, if I'm being serious…I'd rather keep you holed up here with me a hell of a lot more."

She tossed back her head and laughed.

"So, you don't wanna kick me in the balls for saying that?"

She shook her head. "I respect your honesty. Especially now that I know you're serious and not just trying to get in my pants."

"Oh, I'm definitely trying to get in your pants," I assured her.

She laughed again, this time beckoning me closer with her index finger.

I walked over, stopping at the side of the bed. She beckoned me even closer. I bent down so we were at eye level. "Maybe when you get back you can show me what you had in mind."

"Seriously? Are you trying to kill me?"

She tucked her lips to stop from laughing and shook her head.

"You don't say something like that to a guy right before he needs to get ready to leave."

"Why not?"

I grabbed her hand and moved it to the crotch of my boxers. "This is not how I want to show up for my first night on the job."

She squeezed my dick gently, gliding her hand up and down the hardened length of it, sending my body into overdrive.

I wanted her to keep at it. *God, I wanted her to keep at it.* But I needed to get ready to go. I needed to be on time. I needed to show I was responsible enough to hold down a job.

I stared down at her, contemplating the right move.

What was five minutes?

I sprang forward and climbed on top of her, crushing her body into the mattress. Her yelp was captured by my lips. And for the next five minutes, I didn't let her come up for air, making it perfectly clear if I'd be left hot and bothered all night, so would she.

* * *

By two in the morning, I realized why the job working security in the psych building had still been available. I wanted to pull my fucking hair out. I roamed the dark hallways. I made multiple cups of coffee and sat on the couch in the first-floor library. I checked that doors were closed and locked too many times to count. It was shaping up to be a long few weeks.

I sat down by the front door, kicking my feet up on a table and pulling out my phone. I wondered if Sabrina had fallen asleep after I'd left. I couldn't erase the thought of her from my mind. The whole idea of us was nuts, but I think that's why it worked. She had sass and confidence, and I had that cocky edge girls pretended to hate but really loved. They liked a challenge. And I could definitely be a challenge.

The only thing that could fuck it up for us was reality—the rest of the school returning in three short weeks. Or my teammates returning even sooner for our games.

As if she knew I'd been thinking about her, a text from Sabrina popped up on my screen. **How's work?**

My thumbs pounded away at my screen. **Would be better if you were here.**

Three dots lit up the screen and I eagerly awaited her response. **Funny thing about that…**

I stared down at the screen, but another text didn't appear.

A light tapping sounded on the front door.

I stood from my chair and glanced around the empty entranceway. I squinted through the glass door into the darkness outside. A smile spread across my lips. Sabrina stood there wearing my hockey jersey and skinny jeans. I unlocked the door and pushed it open. "Well aren't you the hottest thing I've ever seen."

She smiled as she stepped inside, brushing by me. The scent of her peach body lotion trailed her, working its way into every one of my senses. "Is it okay I'm here?"

I locked the door behind her and turned around.

She'd sat down on the table my feet had been resting on.

"No one here but you, me, and the skulls on the fifth floor." I walked over and stopped in front of her so she had to look up to see me. "I kinda missed you."

Her brows arched. "You kinda missed me? I would've thought having my scent all over you would've been driving you wild."

I chuckled as I cupped her cheeks and leaned closer. "Been driving me more than wild." I seized her lips in a long, eager kiss. It was clear we'd both been starved for it. I dropped my hands to her ass and lifted her off the table. She wrapped her arms around my neck and linked her ankles around my back, driving the kiss deeper. We were all lips and tongue and teeth. This pent-up frustration wasn't going to last much longer. Even with the reprieve earlier, I needed to be inside her. I needed to feel her body tighten around me. I needed to taste her breasts and suck on her nipples. I walked to the closest wall and braced her against it.

She moved against the erection in my jeans. She was as desperate as I was, willing to show up in the middle of the night to get it. She pulled out of the kiss, her breathing labored and her words choppy. "When are you done here?"

I closed my eyes, knowing I had four more hours. "Six."

She huffed. "I can wait if you can?"

"I can't wait."

She laughed as she moved her hands to my face, her fingertips trailing gently over the stubble on my jawline. "I can be strong for the both of us," she assured me.

"Then you need to get outta here. Cuz I'm having difficulty holding off any longer."

Her smile broadened.

I glanced to the front door and the darkness outside. "I don't like the idea of sending you back out in the middle of the night alone."

"We never would've met if I wasn't walking alone in the middle of the night."

I hated the reminder of that night. What had been done to me. How I treated Sabrina. How things went south so quickly. "That was different."

"I'll tell you what. Let's talk all the way home. Then you'll know I got back to your dorm safe and sound."

I stared into her pretty eyes, looking for the assurance that she'd be okay. I placed her down on her feet. If anyone was safe on her own, it was Sabrina. "Deal."

My jersey fell to her knees, but she reached underneath and pulled her phone from her pocket. Mine rang on the table.

I reached for it and, though she stood a few feet away from me, I answered it. "When I get back to the dorm, I want you in my bed in nothing but my jersey."

She smirked as she spoke into her phone. "Deal."

Sabrina

The chill of the night air prickled my skin as I made my way down the steps with my phone to my ear. "No crazy slashers around," I informed Crosby as I glanced from side to side.

"What is it with you and slashers?" he laughed. "You thought I was hiding a machete the night we met."

I smiled, amazed by how safe I felt hearing his voice as I moved along the dark path. "What'd you expect? I couldn't see you."

"Then I certainly gave you an eye full."

I laughed. "That's an understatement."

His laughter carried through the phone causing butterflies to dance in my belly.

"Do you know how hard it was to keep my eyes from staring at your package. I'd had a shitty night and was buzzed, so my resolve was pretty weak."

He laughed again. "From here on out I give you full permission to stare all you want. Same goes for touching and tasting. Go crazy."

"You're such a guy."

"Yup. Are you almost back to the dorm?"

I looked around. Getting lost in our conversation, I'd only made it a few buildings down from the psychology building where he worked. "Almost," I lied.

"Thanks for coming to see me." The thoughtfulness in his voice was still so strange for me given our rough start. It was like Crosby and Mr. Hockey *were* two totally different people. So different yet so alike.

I stopped mid-stride. I knew I'd never be able to sleep alone in Crosby's room without him, especially now that I knew what awaited me upon his return.

"You there?" he asked.

"I'm here." I turned back around and jogged toward the psychology building, with my heart racing in my chest. Sure, I usually talked a big game, but when the time came to throw caution to the wind, I thought twice about it. At least I usually did. Tonight, all bets were off. It only took a minute to reach the steps. I stopped at the bottom and stared at the glass door.

"Why do you sound out of breath?" Crosby asked.

I climbed the steps and stood in front of the door for the second time that night. I tapped on it.

"What the hell?" Crosby mumbled into the phone. I could hear his footsteps through the phone. And then he appeared in the door. A wide smile spread across his face once again. He unlocked the door and pushed it open. "Forget something?"

"I'm not gonna be able to wait." I launched myself forward, wrapping my arms around his neck.

He stumbled back, my kiss silencing his surprise. He dropped his hands to my ass and picked me up. I wrapped my legs around his hips like earlier. But this was different. This was more frantic. More urgent. More…everything.

I wanted him and I wanted him right there.

And given the way his mouth moved in tandem with mine, it *was* happening right there. He walked us down the dark hallway, never releasing my lips. He was on a mission. And I was gladly along for the ride.

He turned into a dark room—a library. He walked us toward the sofa in the center of the room and lowered me onto it. He stood over me. "God, you're so hot in my jersey."

My chest rose and fell with each breath.

The room was dark, but I couldn't miss the hunger in his eyes. "But I need to see you out of it."

My lips kicked up in the corners. "There's Mr. Hockey."

He smirked as I pushed up onto my elbows and lifted his jersey over my head, leaving me in my lacy black bra. His breath hitched as he stared down at me. His eyes moved over my chest, the widening in his eyes the approval I didn't realize I needed. He reached behind his neck and pulled his shirt over his head, tossing it to the floor.

I'd seen him shirtless before. But the way his jeans hung low on his hips with his boxers peeking out quickened my pulse.

His eyes stayed on mine as his fingers moved to the button on his jeans. He slipped it through the slot then pushed his jeans and boxers down his legs. "Nothing you haven't seen before."

My eyes lowered. He was right. I'd seen all of him before. But now I had the chance to take him all in. Every. Last. Inch.

He stepped toward me, the corded muscles in his thighs so pronounced. Hockey looked good on him. He bent over me and reached for the button on my jeans, slipping it through the slot and tugging my jeans down my legs and off with my sneakers. He gazed down at me sprawled out on the sofa in my lacy thong and matching bra. "Better than I imagined," he said as he covered me with his body.

We'd been like this before, but my towel and his boxers separated us. This was intimate. This was raw. This was what we both needed.

"There's no way I can be gentle right now," he said, his lips inches from mine.

"Thank God," I breathed.

He reached for my wrists and wrapped his massive hand around them, pinning my arms above my head. He kissed his way down my body with slow, torturous, open-mouthed kisses that left tremors in their wake and set my body abuzz.

This was going to be so much better than *I* imagined.

"Don't move them," he said as his hands left my wrists, drifted down my arms, and slipped around to my back. He unsnapped the clasp on my bra and pulled the straps up my arms, twisting them around my wrists to keep me bound. He gazed down at me for a long time. I wasn't easily embarrassed, but his slow appraisal had goosebumps popping up all over my skin. "How's it feel to be the one tied up?"

"Are you gonna set me free?"

His lips slipped into a slow cocky smirk. "Not right now I'm not."

Tingles spread out to parts of my body I didn't realize were erogenous zones.

"I don't even know where to start," he said, his eyes moving over me again.

"I didn't take you for someone who lacked experience in this department."

His brows shot up, amusement playing behind his eyes. "Oh, I've got experience. I just don't know what to do first to let your body know it belongs to me tonight."

I swallowed down my fervor.

"Fuck it." He reached down and tore my panties down my legs. He didn't waste time appreciating my naked body spread out before him. He grabbed for his jeans and snatched a condom from his wallet. He rolled it on and within seconds he'd found my entrance. He promised rough, but he moved the tip over my swollen skin gently. "You're already so wet."

My eyes pinched tight, appreciating the feel of him but anticipating his size.

"God, I've been waiting for this."

I opened my eyes. "I'm not going anywhere."

"No, you're not," he assured me, pushing inside with one hard thrust.

My back arched off the sofa. His rhythm started slow but each thrust became faster and harder. I needed to be closer. I needed to feel him. I slipped my bound wrists over his head. But that wasn't enough. I needed him deeper. I wrapped my ankles behind his ass as he continued his pursuit. I'd had sex before but never had a guy hit that spot. The one that made you cross-eyed when he grazed it. Crosby knew where it was. And each time he reared back and thrust in, he hit it. Each time sending zingers ricocheting through my body.

My eyes squeezed shut as I relished in the feel of him. The strength of his body pinning me beneath him. The solidity of him stretching me wide. *Gah.* I felt him everywhere.

He buried his face in the crook of my neck, assaulting me with sloppy open-mouthed kisses. He may have been in shape from hockey, but his ragged breaths told me this moment was giving him a much-needed release.

My insides began to twist and coil. "Oh, God."

"You there?" he asked, his thrusts getting harder and deeper.

"*Yesssss.*" Everything between my thighs tightened, and a suppressed ball of energy exploded down to my toes. My entire body hummed.

With a few more determined grunts and thrusts, Crosby followed me over the edge, releasing a long deep groan into my neck.

I tightened my grasp on him and relished in the feel of him in my arms.

Eventually, he lowered himself down on top of me. We both lay there, our deep breaths mirroring each other's. We said nothing, enjoying the after tremors and silence that surrounded us.

After some time, Crosby lifted his head and rested his chin on my chest. "If you told me it would be that good, there's no way I would've pissed you off so much."

"I think *because* you pissed me off it was that good."

He scoffed. "Well, then. I think you look fat."

I laughed, but my laughter was silenced by the softness of his lips and the slow glide of his tongue as he kissed me. He was saying what neither of us wanted to say. What we were too stubborn to say. This thing between us could be real.

Now that the sex was out of the way, we were still connected and I kinda liked that we were. And given the gentleness of this kiss, he liked it too.

CHAPTER SIXTEEN

Sabrina

Crosby and I sat cuddled under a blanket on the sofa in the psych building—our new favorite spot. The tablet we'd propped up on the table in front of us displayed the tightly-packed crowd in Time's Square anxiously awaiting the new year just minutes away. People wore elaborate hats and glasses and were bundled up for the frigid twenty-degree weather outside. I'd take the warmth of Crosby's body any day.

Four days had passed since our night on the same sofa. And Crosby remained the same. Fun. Considerate. Kind. Had it been me showing up on campus or the hot sex we'd been having multiple times a day that caused the transformation? I liked to believe I brought out the best in him, because I'd definitely seen him at his worst.

Crosby pulled me closer into him. "What are you thinking?"

"Just how crazy life can be."

"Agreed."

The people on the screen grew more excited over the impending ball drop, kissing for the camera or waving to family members back home.

"Did you have a lot of girlfriends back in Texas?"

Crosby snickered. "Where'd that come from?"

"Just wondering."

He shrugged. "I wouldn't call them girlfriends."

"So, no one special?"

"You asking if you're my girlfriend?"

"What? No. I was just curious what you were like?"

He pulled in a breath then released it slowly, saying nothing.

Had bringing up the past ruined the mood? Set him on edge? Pissed him off? *Damage control.* "I'll tell you what I picture. I picture you strutting across campus with a hoard of girls following you around hoping for a mere glance from your pretty blue eyes."

He laughed. "Let's get one thing straight. I don't strut."

"Fine. Saunter. You sauntered across campus." I laughed. "I also picture all the other guys on campus wanting to be you. You know, bumping your fist when you passed them in the hallways and calling you Bro whenever you entered a room in hopes that you'd wanna grab a beer or chill with them at their frat."

"They certainly didn't wanna tie me to a tree."

My heart clenched at the reminder of all the life changes he'd endured in such a short period of time. "I'm sorry it sucks that much for you here."

He turned his head and looked me in the eyes. "It doesn't suck so much anymore."

His sexy tone of voice mixed with the implied meaning of his words brought ripples between my thighs. And the searing look in his eyes told me what he wanted. What *I* wanted. But I needed to distract him if we were going to see the countdown and ring in the new year together. "So, you planning on making any New Year's resolutions?"

The sexy way he chewed on his bottom lip was a true testament to the consideration he gave my question. My eyes zeroed in on his teeth worrying his lip, knowing exactly what that lip tasted like. What those teeth felt like when they nipped at my skin. "I'm not sure. You?"

I tilted my head, considering the upcoming year and all I planned to accomplish. "I think I'm gonna declare a major."

"Pre-law?"

I smiled. "How'd you know?"

"You are the most stubborn and determined girl I've ever met."

I laughed. "And you love it."

"I don't hate it, that's for sure."

My stomach fluttered at the assurance in his tone. "I know a resolution for you."

He arched a brow. "You're making my resolutions for me now?"

I dislodged myself from his arm and climbed into his lap, straddling him so I could look him in the eyes. "I think you need to spend all your free time making me happy."

His head fell back as a laugh tumbled out of him. "Oh, that's it?"

"That's it."

"And how am I gonna do that?"

I leaned forward and pressed my mouth to his. The aftertaste of hot cocoa and the sound of the countdown on the television welcomed us into the new year as we spent the remainder of the night in each other's arms.

If that was an indication of what the new year would be like, the future looked increasingly bright for both of us.

CHAPTER SEVENTEEN

January

Sabrina

From my spot in the passenger seat, I glanced over at Crosby driving with one hand resting on the top of my steering wheel, so comfortable driving my car. His tattoos shone so vibrantly in the bright Saturday morning sun.

"I can't wait to see you play."

His eyes cut to mine before jumping between the deserted stretch of Louisiana road and me. "You've already seen me play."

"That doesn't really count."

"Why not?"

"I wasn't there for you," I explained. "Or at least I was only there to piss you off."

He threw back his head and howled with laughter. "Seriously?"

"Maybe."

He shook his head in disbelief. "When I saw you there, I just couldn't understand what you'd see in Jeremy."

"I gave him a shot." I shrugged. "He turned out to be a jerk."

"I think he only asked you out to get to me."

"Hence the jerk."

"You knew?"

"His grilling at dinner about my meeting with the dean tipped me off," I explained.

"He wanted to know if you ratted them out?"

I nodded. "And him sending me to your room proved it was all about you."

Crosby shook his head. "He's such a douche."

I glanced out the window at the passing signs. "You weren't much better. Just saying."

He reached over and linked his fingers with mine, resting them in my lap. "I'll make it up to you."

"Is that a threat or a promise?"

"Do you have a comment for everything?"

My eyes shifted back over at him. "Anything worth saying."

His eyes remained on the road. "You're pretty fantastic."

"Keep going."

His smile grew. "And sexy."

"And?"

"And when are you coming to a game to watch *me*?"

"January twelfth is an away game. So whichever game is after that."

His smile reached all the way to his eyes. "You know when my next game is?"

"I looked it up when I was trying to figure out when you'd be back at school."

"That when you realized I never left?"

I nodded. "No more holidays alone. Okay?"

His eyes cut to mine and his smile turned me into the type of giddy girl I swore I'd never be.

* * *

Crosby stepped out of the hotel bathroom in nothing but a towel hanging low on his hips.

I drank him in, wondering if the water droplets rolling down his chest were meant to distract me—anything to avoid visiting his father. And if he kept staring at me with those hungry eyes, I might've let him blow off his visit so we could spend the day in bed. But it had been months since he'd spoken to his dad. He needed to.

Trying to distract him—and have a little fun of my own—I held up my phone and snapped a few pictures of him.

He laughed as he moved forward, each step displaying more of his body.

My phone rang. It was Finlay. I sent it to voicemail and snapped more pictures, capturing each predatory step he took closer to me.

"Who was that?"

"Finlay." *Click.*

"You sent it to voicemail?"

I nodded. *Click. Click.*

"What's she think about me bringing you to Texas?"

"I didn't tell her." *Click.*

He stopped, eyeing me curiously. "Why not?"

I shrugged.

He leaned against the dresser and crossed his arms.

"Nice. Stay like that." I took a couple more pictures, but he wasn't smiling.

"Wait a minute. Does she even know about us?"

Trying to ignore his question, I checked the pictures to be sure they were focused.

"She doesn't, does she?" The surprise in his voice caused me to cringe.

I forced my eyes up. "I'm not ready to hear her say, 'I told you so.'"

A smug grin slipped across his lips. "I guess you should've listened to her then."

I cocked my head, not needing to hear it from him either.

He walked over to the bed and sat beside me, the mattress drooping beneath his weight. He leaned over and his wet hair brushed against my cheek as he peppered my neck and collarbone with kisses. "Any way I can convince you that I don't need to go?"

I shook my head.

His gentle kisses turned to open-mouthed kisses. "I could be persuaded to drop the towel for a few more pictures."

"What's the point? I can search online and find plenty."

Without missing a beat, he pinned me beneath him on the bed. His body held me in place as water droplets from his hair dripped onto my face. "That was cold, woman."

I giggled, loving the way his face relaxed when he looked into my eyes. "You need to go," I said.

He closed his eyes and nodded.

"I'll wait in the car for as long as you need me to."

He inched closer. "Thank you."

Crosby

My mother's prison had been a day spa compared to the hellhole my father now resided in. It was the type of place you saw in movies. Century-old rusted bars crisscrossed the small windows on the cobblestone exterior. Barbwire circled the tops of the multiple fences surrounding the building. And misery plagued the faces of guards and visitors in the drab gray waiting room where I sat completely unprepared to come face to face with the man I hated.

"Parks," a guard called.

I jumped to my feet and followed him through a locked door into a room filled with old wooden tables and chairs. My father sat at a table with his back to me. My shoes suddenly became cement blocks, dragging the closer I got to him. Why had I decided to do this? Why had I let Sabrina convince me it was something I needed to do?

I slipped into the seat across from him. Prison had aged him. That or his weekly trips to the spa had concealed the aging man now seated before me. One with hard lines around his eyes and gray wisps of hair around his ears. "Hi."

His emotionless eyes stared back at me. "I didn't think you'd come."

"I hadn't planned on it."

He nodded. "You were always closer with your mother."

I didn't argue the fact. Seemed like a moot point. He'd been a cold son of a bitch who never invested time in me.

"Have you spoken to her?" he asked, though given the offhandedness in his tone, I wondered if he actually cared.

"She calls almost every day. I saw her on Thanksgiving and I'm heading there tomorrow."

"I suppose you didn't see me because I don't call," he said with the snide condescension I'd grown up expecting from him.

"I suppose," I said.

"So, what's changed? I don't have any money to give you."

I scoffed. "You think I'm here for money?"

"Aren't you?"

"You've got nothing left. You know that, right?"

He lifted his chin and looked away, as if he still possessed the tiniest shred of dignity in a place like that.

It took everything in me not to say, 'Come on, dude. You shower and piss in front of other guys.'

His eyes cut back to mine. "So, why *are* you here?"

"Just thought it was the right thing to do." My attention drifted to a couple a few tables over. The woman was pregnant. I wondered if their unborn kid was better off being born with a father in prison instead of having him at home teaching him the wrong way to grow up. My eyes ventured back to my father. "Thanks for hiding the business side of things from me."

"What's that supposed to mean?"

"It's better that I didn't know what you were doing. I'll be okay not having money. I wouldn't have been okay if I watched you steal from innocent people. Knowing I had no knowledge of it helps deal with the anger toward our family." I watched him closely. Watched to see if he even cared my life had been affected by his decisions. But his blank stare continued.

"So, you're thanking me?"

"In a screwed-up kind of way, I guess I am." I stared down at the handcuffs wrapped around his wrists. I didn't need to look away from them like I did my mom's. For some reason, it wasn't odd to see them there.

"Still playing hockey?"

"At Alabama now."

His head flinched back. "What? Why?"

If he didn't understand the trail of disaster he'd left in his wake, I didn't have the energy to explain it to him. "Just thought it was for the best."

"Your mother arrange that?"

I nodded.

"Of course she did," he muttered. "Well, keep focused on your goal and stay healthy. That way you can go early in the draft."

"I intend to."

"I've seen those contracts. You're gonna be a very wealthy man. Just be careful. Women will be crawling out of the woodwork for you, wanting to get their claws on your money. Be safe." He nodded toward the pregnant woman at the other table. "They'll do anything to hold onto you."

"You think money's the only reason someone would want to be with me?"

"Absolutely. Money's all anyone sees."

"You should know, huh?"

He looked away, the accuracy of my words pissing him off. Too bad I didn't care.

The pregnant woman's chair scraped on the floor, and she pushed herself slowly to her feet. She wiped a tear from her eye as she turned and walked away from the inmate still seated at the table.

I pulled my attention away from the sad scene and looked back at my father. "It's not about the money for me."

A derisive laugh shot from his lips. "You say that now."

I shook my head. "Nope. I'm not you. All I need is a stick and skates and I'll be okay."

"Call me in a few years if hockey doesn't work out. I'd love to hear if your ideals have changed."

"Deal."

Sabrina

"So that's what a power play is?" I said, dipping a tortilla chip into the spicy bowl of salsa we shared.

"Yup," Crosby said, sipping his beer in the Mexican restaurant he'd picked. Apparently, Texans loved their Mexican food.

The colorful décor and soft mariachi music surrounding us proved to be the perfect balance for an otherwise difficult day for Crosby—at least, I assumed it was difficult. He hadn't spoken a word about his time with his dad. After his visit, he returned to the car where I waited and kissed me long and hard. I was convinced he was trying to rid himself of the past and lose himself in the normalcy of what we'd been creating.

"Do you know what a hat trick is?" he asked.

I shook my head.

He smiled, but I could see he was trying not to make me feel stupid for asking what I assumed to be a ridiculous question. "Three goals in one game by a single player."

"This hockey stuff isn't so tough," I said, popping another tortilla chip into my mouth.

"Says the girl who can't skate."

I laughed with my mouth full. "Can, too."

His eyes dropped to my mouth. "You with a mouthful is a good look."

I rolled my eyes as I swallowed the last of my bite. "Smooth."

He laughed. "I thought you like it when Mr. Hockey makes an appearance?"

I did. But I still wanted to know how it went with his dad. "So—"

"It was fine," Crosby said, cutting me off.

"I'm here if you wanna talk about it."

"I know."

My brows shot up. "Do you?"

Sadness clouded his eyes. "I'm trying."

"Well, promise me you'll at least talk to your mom about it in the morning."

He nodded.

Our waiter approached with a tray piled high with food, interrupting our conversation and lighting up Crosby's eyes.

The waiter placed the dish Crosby ordered for me in front of me.

"Looks good, right?" Crosby said, eagerly scooping up something that looked like a taco from his own dish as soon as the waiter placed it down.

"Sure. You gonna tell me what I should start with?"

He lifted the food in his hand. "The puffy taco."

I picked up the puffy taco from my dish and examined it.

He laughed. "I can't believe you've never had a puffy taco before."

"I can't believe how much it makes me want to laugh every time I hear you say 'puffy taco.'"

He laughed before taking a big bite, eating nearly half of it.

I followed his lead, biting into mine but taking a much smaller bite to gauge if I liked it. The puffy taco shell added a dough-like texture to the outside, while the warm gooey inside set my taste buds on overdrive. I took another bite, this time getting more of the tasty goodness inside.

"Good, right?"

I nodded, chewing down the delicious food.

"I like having you here."

My nose wrinkled. "In a Mexican restaurant?"

He snickered. "No. In my home state…It feels right."

"You wanna stop by your old school so you can show me off?"

He grinned.

"Is that a yes or a no?"

"It's a yes to wanting to show you off but no to going to my old campus." His phone buzzed on the table, but he didn't reach for it. He just lifted his glass and sipped his beer.

"Aren't you gonna get it?"

"Who's more important than you?" he asked.

"Wow. Get you started and the lines just keep on rolling."

He laughed as he placed down his glass and grabbed his phone. Surprise washed over his features as he stared down at the screen.

"What is it?"

He held up his phone so I could read the text. **A scout will be at our next home game to see you play.**

"Is that from your coach?"

He nodded.

"That's amazing."

A smile inched across his face. "That's *fucking* amazing."

My head dropped back and I laughed. Like really laughed.

Whether he wanted to talk about his father or not, Crosby was going to be okay. This was his time, and he was going to crush it for that scout.

CHAPTER EIGHTEEN

Sabrina

With the majority of campus still on winter recess, the bar wasn't as packed as usual. Small groups of people milled around, but a few high-top tables were empty. I sat alone at one, my foot bouncing anxiously on the stool rung while I stared down at Finlay's text. She and Caden would be there in five minutes.

The football team had just returned after winning their bowl game. Now they needed to prepare like crazy for their upcoming championship game in Georgia. But for the time being, I had my best friend back. At least, back on campus. I hadn't seen her yet. She was unpacking her things at Caden's since our dorm was still closed.

"Dance with me," Crosby said against my ear, his minty breath sending chills up and down my arms.

I turned to find his blue eyes dancing playfully as he placed our drinks down on the table. "I'm having a strange case of déjà vu right now," I said, stifling a smile.

I hopped down from my stool, and he guided me with his hands on my hips onto the dance floor. Beneath the dim lights, he slipped his arms around me and pulled me flush against his chest.

I wrapped my arms around his neck and we began moving to the slow song filtering into the bar.

"I've been wanting to make it up to you for the last time we were out here," Crosby said.

"Why? I liked being out here with you."

His head shot back. "Bullshit."

I shook my head, my eyes never wavering from his. "I think I was fighting what I was feeling that night so damn hard I just needed you to do something to get me to leave."

His lips curved, loving my admission.

The song switched to a fast song and Crosby grabbed my hand and lifted it over my head, twirling me around the nearly empty dance floor. I threw back my head and laughed, loving that this was the first time people were seeing us together and Crosby looked happy. He *was* happy. And so was I. He kept my hand in his grasp and tugged me back into him. I wrapped my arms around his neck as his arms slipped around my hips. But something changed on his face as his eyes lifted over my shoulder.

"What's wrong?" I asked.

"They're here."

My heart drummed a little faster in my chest, but I didn't turn around. "Are they looking?"

"Yup."

I slipped my hands to the back of his head, burying my fingers in his hair. Before I could urge his mouth down, his lips were already moving over mine. I hated public displays, but being on the receiving end of Crosby's felt amazing.

I pulled out of the kiss and glanced over my shoulder at Finlay and Caden, staring with their mouths open. Crosby grabbed hold of my hand and walked me back to the table.

"You've both got some explaining to do," Finlay said, a mix of amusement and anger playing in her eyes. Caden sat down beside her letting her do all the talking.

I slipped onto my stool. "Ummm."

"Let's just say she couldn't resist Mr. Hockey anymore," Crosby explained, slipping onto the stool beside me.

I rolled my eyes at him. "You're so ridiculous."

"Only about you, baby."

"Ugh," I groaned. "Don't make me go back to hating you."

"I thought we already agreed you never hated me. You've wanted my body since the day you laid eyes on it."

Caden looked disgusted while Finlay smiled, her eyes jumping between the two of us. "I like this."

"What?" I asked.

"The two of you. It makes me happy," she said.

"It makes me happier," Crosby said. "The girl can't get enough of me."

I shoved him so hard, I practically knocked him off his stool.

"Nice, Sabrina," Caden said. "Keep him in line."

Crosby looked to me. "Am I lying?"

Finlay laughed. "This keeps getting better and better."

"You got that right," Crosby said, his words meant for Finlay, but I knew he was referring to what was happening between us.

And I had to agree with him.

Since I arrived back on campus, each day had only gotten better.

* * *

The chill in the arena wrenched my breath out of me in white puffy clouds as I watched Crosby zigzag all over the empty ice with the puck at the end of his stick. He'd been practicing and working his butt off since he found out a scout would be at his next home game. He was determined to be at his best. Determined to stand out. And by the looks of it, he had nothing to worry about.

I'd seen him naked on more than one occasion, but the sight of him on the ice, moving with such grace and determination, was so damn hot. The way his legs carried him effortlessly across the rink. The way his arms maneuvered the stick as if it weighed nothing at all. The way he spun and swerved while remaining on his skates. A guy with those moves just knew what to do with his body, and I freaking loved it.

He skated to the side and stopped in front of the bench area where I sat alone. "Hey."

"You look good out there."

His cocky grin—the one I was becoming all too familiar with—slipped into place. "I look good everywhere."

I groaned, secretly enjoying his cockiness.

He laughed. "Stop acting like you don't love it."

I stared him right in the eyes. "I don't love it."

"Don't make me throw you over my shoulder again."

My eyes widened as I grabbed hold of the edge of the bench beneath me. "You wouldn't."

He stepped up into the bench area, towering over me on his skates. "Try me."

"There's a fine line between sexy and arrogant."

"Glad to hear I've mastered both."

I rolled my eyes.

"You ready to get outta here?" he relented. "I've gotta get to work."

"Sure."

"Let me go drop off my stuff and I'll meet you by the door."

"You sure you don't need help?" I asked with bouncing brows.

"You trying to kill me?"

"Kill you? No. Get in *your* pants. Yes."

He laughed as he stepped back onto the ice and skated to the locker room.

I sat for a little while enjoying the quiet in the arena. I couldn't wait to be there with the place packed with fans so I could cheer on Crosby. It was a heady feeling to know the guy on the ice was the guy I got to see at his sexiest. At his most vulnerable. At his best.

A bout of sadness swept over me. His teammates would be returning tomorrow to get a practice in before they traveled to Tennessee the following day. Our time on the deserted campus would be over and reality would set in. And that sucked. I'd gotten used to having the place to ourselves. To having Crosby to myself. To having no one around to ruin what we had.

I eventually stood and moved to the entrance. The pitter-patter of raindrops hit the glass doors. I stared out into the dark night. The rain came down hard, bouncing off the empty parking lot and creating puddles everywhere. I pushed open the door and stepped out into it. The bitter air mixing with the cold drops pricked the hairs on my arms.

"What are you doing?" Crosby asked, stepping outside behind me.

I glanced over my shoulder as he pulled off his sweatshirt. He held it above me, trying to create an umbrella. I ducked away from him and twirled around the parking lot with my arms spread wide and my face upward.

"It's fifty degrees out here," he called over the spray of rain.

I closed my eyes and continued to twirl, enjoying the solace of the rainstorm. "Doesn't mean I can't enjoy the rain."

His arms unexpectedly slipped around my waist from behind and he lifted me off my feet. I giggled, enjoying not only the rain, but Crosby sharing the moment with me.

"Do that again," he murmured into the side of my neck.

"Do what?"

"Laugh."

I craned my neck to look at him over my shoulder. "I laugh all the time."

"But you did it because of something I did. I want to make you laugh all the time." He twisted me in his arms. My hands landed on his shoulders before slipping around his neck. Our soaked bodies pressed against each other. "Sorry I didn't before."

"Before, you didn't know me." I lifted my hands to his cold flushed cheeks. "Now you do."

He smiled, and the candidness in his smile dipped my belly. I pulled his lips down to mine and kissed him slow and soft, quite a contrast to the cold seeping into our skin and the rain ricocheting off our bodies. My tongue dipped inside his mouth, so warm and inviting. His fingers tunneled into my hair as he held me tighter, deepening the kiss in the empty parking lot in the middle of a rainstorm.

Our breathing was ragged when I pulled out of the kiss. "I want more moments like this with you," I said.

"Done."

I grinned. "Is everything that easy with you?"

"Yup."

My head fell back and I laughed, the rain jabbing my face yet again. This time I slipped free of Crosby's grasp and took off running. "Race you home," I called over my shoulder.

"I'm already home," he called.

I stopped and turned back to face him. His feet remained planted in the same spot where I'd left him. What he'd said and the smitten look in his eyes sent a shiver through my already chilled body. I swallowed hard. "So, you're not coming?"

He pushed his soaked hair away from his face as he took a couple steps toward me. "I'm coming. I was just admiring your ass. I need something to get me through those long nights in Tennessee."

"You'll be gone for *one* night."

"One night with you on my mind and Tennessee's ass in the palm of my hand."

"What is it with you and asses?"

He stopped in front of me and looked down with raindrops hanging from his long eyelashes. "Don't worry. I don't discriminate. I like every part of your body."

I slipped my arms around his waist and stared up at him. "The feeling's mutual."

CHAPTER NINETEEN

Crosby

I tried Sabrina's phone as soon as I entered the visitors' locker room after our victory over Tennessee. I couldn't wait to tell her about my two goals, but she wasn't answering her phone.

I hopped in the shower, hoping there'd be a message waiting by the time I got out. I hadn't realized how starved I was for someone to talk to about hockey. Sure, my mom asked about my games when we spoke, but having Sabrina now, someone to get all excited for me and share in my excitement, was something I hadn't realized I needed.

I stepped back into the locker room drying off from my shower. Some of the guys were already dressed and heading to the bus. Jeremy stood at his locker in a towel, hovering over his phone with a couple of other guys. They laughed at something on the screen.

Jeremy's eyes lifted from the phone and his glare met mine.

My eyes narrowed. Had the assholes gone and recorded me in the shower? I was starting to think they liked seeing me naked.

"You and Sabrina have fun over break?" Jeremy asked.

I cocked my head. "Come again?"

He shrugged. "Just saying it must've been nice having the whole campus to yourselves. What'd you two crazy kids do?"

A cold fear spread over me. Why was he asking? How did he know? Knowing better than to let him see he got to me, I played it off as if it didn't bother me. "You jealous, Potter?"

"Of the whore?"

"Fuck you," I spat.

He laughed, glancing around at his friends before looking back to me. "Careful," he warned. "Wouldn't want the scout catching wind of your poor attitude."

I glared at him, wanting to level him right there and then. But I knew everything out of his mouth was a calculated effort to get to me. I *wouldn't* make it easy for him.

I grabbed my things and dressed alone in the restroom, wanting to avoid another run-in with Jeremy. But as we drove through the night back to Alabama, Jeremy's words haunted me. The fact that he brought up Sabrina sent up warning signs. He'd already asked her out to get to me; what was his point in bringing her up now? Why make it clear he knew we were alone together on campus? *Was* he jealous I was with her now? Or was there an underlying threat to his comments?

I tried Sabrina's cell throughout the bus ride home. But she never answered or responded, and for some reason that scared the hell out of me.

* * *

It wasn't quite dawn as I pounded on Sabrina's door. Her dorm had reopened, and I'd likely woken whoever was back on her floor in the process. But I needed to see her. I'd sprinted across campus as soon as I stepped off the team bus, needing to know she was okay.

I heard the click of the door unlocking. My heart squeezed in my chest. Sabrina opened the door, her eyes sleepy and her hair a tangled mess.

I lunged forward, grasping her cheeks in my hand and kissing her hard.

She pulled back with a confused look. "Miss me?"

"God, yeah." My eyes jumped around her room. Finlay's bed was made and empty. I kicked the door shut behind me and walked Sabrina backward until I lowered her onto her bed and covered her with my body. "Why didn't you answer your phone?"

"It died and I couldn't find my charger. I think I left it at your place."

I closed my eyes and buried my nose in her hair, breathing her in. "Are you okay?"

"Yeah. Why?"

"Jeremy said something about us being on campus alone, and I didn't know what he was getting at," I said. "I just needed to be sure you were okay."

I felt her body tense beneath me.

I pulled back enough to see her tired eyes. "What's wrong?"

"I need to tell you something," she said hesitantly.

"Okay."

"I kind of threatened Jeremy before break."

My eyes narrowed. "What do you mean you kind of threatened him?"

"At the bar. Before you and I danced. I told him I'd go to the dean about what he did to you. He got all scary-looking and said I wouldn't want to start something I couldn't stop."

"Sabrina," I sighed, unable to believe she'd stood up to him for me—especially since she'd pretty much hated me before break. "I don't need you fighting my battles."

"It wasn't about you. I provoked him," she said.

Had she? Because at this point, I had no idea what he was capable of. All I knew was he hated me and he seemed like he'd do anything to get me to quit the team. "You can't blame yourself for anything he does. You hear me?"

She nodded.

"Thanks for trying to stand up to him for me, though."

She smiled and that smile made anything Jeremy said seem unimportant now.

* * *

Practice wasn't as brutal that night. Jeremy wasn't up to his normal antics. If anything, he stayed away from me. Maybe he realized I was done being made to look like a fool.

I showered and packed up my gear, hurrying out of the arena and heading for Sabrina's. Finlay was staying at Caden's again, so we had the room to ourselves.

I made my way outside and began my trek to her dorm. Half-way there, my phone vibrated in my pocket. I slipped it out, figuring it would be a text from Sabrina. It wasn't. It was a link from an anonymous sender. My curiosity got the best of me and I clicked the link.

A shiver of dread scampered up my spine as a grainy video played on the screen.

I stopped, holding the phone closer. My pulse pounded in my temples as I stood helplessly watching a video of Sabrina and me having sex in the psych building. The recording wasn't from a surveillance camera. It was from someone's phone. Though we'd been in the dark library, I could clearly see it was us. The sounds coming from the recording were those filled with pleasure, but the only feeling rushing through my body while watching it was fear.

Fucking Jeremy.

Had he been there? Had he recorded us? And who else had seen the video? Who else had it?

Tears stung my eyes. Fucking tears. Sabrina had been brought into my mess. She was being targeted *because* of me.

I shoved my phone into my pocket and dragged my shaking fingers through my hair. My world was spiraling and I had no idea how to stop it. Sabrina's reputation hung in the balance and there wasn't a damn thing I could do. I was at Jeremy's mercy. He knew it and I knew it.

Students crisscrossed the campus heading to and from their classes and the dorms. Were they all looking at me? Had they already seen the video? Strangely, I wasn't worried about me. They'd all seen *me* naked. I was worried about Sabrina. About what they'd say about her. How they'd treat her.

My guilty heart raced. This was all my fault. I'd brought her into this. How would she ever be able to forgive me if she found out?

She wouldn't.

* * *

Xavier sat at my desk, his laptop, tablet, and phone all running searches for the video. He'd sworn up and down he had no knowledge of it. He was the only guy on the team who'd been decent to me—reaching outcast status by hanging with me. I owed it to him to trust him.

I sat on my bed, my phone and tablet both running their own searches. But nothing turned up. It had been two hours since I'd received the video. And being unable to find it gave me hope it was only meant to fuck with me.

My phone pinged and a text from Sabrina popped up. *Shit.* I'd forgotten to text her. **You running late?**

Bile crept up the back of my throat. How did you tell someone her entire world could be ruined by the click of a button? **Sorry. Not feeling well. Don't wanna get you sick.** I texted back like the coward I was.

OMG! The scout's coming 2moro. Get some rest.

I didn't respond to her text. I couldn't.

"Dude. It's not here," Xavier said.

I exhaled a breath, knowing it was just a matter of time before the other shoe dropped.

"I'm gonna head out." He gathered up his devices and stuffed them into his backpack. "But I'll keep the searches going tonight."

I nodded, but it didn't stop my stomach from churning.

"What are you gonna do?" he asked.

"I have no fucking clue. I appreciate your help, man."

"It was nothing. Look, I'll keep my ears open. Let you know if I hear anything."

"Thanks."

He pulled open my door and walked out.

The silence that remained in my room was deafening. I fell back on my bed and scrubbed my palms up and down my face. I was lying to Sabrina. With each passing minute that I didn't tell her about the video, I was keeping something from her that very much involved her. And her future. What kind of person was I?

She deserved better than me.

She deserved to know the truth.

But the truth meant my days were numbered. And the reality was, I was a selfish bastard. And I wasn't ready to let her go yet.

CHAPTER TWENTY

Crosby

I rolled out from under my sheets and placed my bare feet on the floor. I dropped my face into my hands and sat for a long time. I'd barely slept. So many emotions ran through me. Tonight was a huge night for me, but all I could think about was the video. And the revenge I wanted to exact on Jeremy and whoever helped him.

I grabbed my phone from my nightstand and my heart clenched. A text from Sabrina was on the screen. **Hope you're feeling better. I'm so excited 2 see you play 2nite. Good luck!!**

I knew I wouldn't see her today. It was her hectic day with back to back classes and a lab, so she clearly wanted to be sure her text covered everything she would've said in person. Even if we could've found time to meet up, I would've made up an excuse to avoid her. I was too much of a coward to face her. To look her in the eyes, knowing what I knew. And, knowing Sabrina, she would've known something was wrong. She would've grilled me until I told her something.

Again, I didn't text her back. Instead, I searched online for the video and called Xavier to see if he found anything. Neither of us had, which enabled me to breathe—at least for the time being.

* * *

I stormed into the locker room. My teammates were in various stages of dress. Some taped their sticks, some laced their skates, and others finished padding up before Coach's pre-game speech. And, while I'd been dealing with the guilt and anger of a video hanging over me like a guillotine ready to drop, they didn't seem to have a fucking care in the world.

Screw that.

I dropped my bag on the ground. The thud reverberated throughout the room. Eyes cut to mine as I glared at them, my body quaking with rage. How many had been involved? How many had been there to record Sabrina and me? How many of them had the video? The scathing look on my face told them what my words didn't have to. I. Was. Done.

Their guilty eyes evaded mine. Jeremy was the only one with the balls to look back at me.

Xavier stepped out from the bathroom in his shoulder pads. His wide eyes locked on mine. The subtle shake of his head said something I couldn't read. Did he want me to wait until after the game to unleash my rage? Was the coach nearby?

Well, I had news for him—for all of them. There wasn't a chance in hell I was taking this one lying down.

I flew across the room, grabbing Jeremy by the throat and slamming him into the lockers behind him. "Erase the video."

"What?" he choked out.

"I know you have it."

"What are you talking about?" His eyes flashed from side to side, desperate for his buddies to intervene. They didn't.

I turned to look at their stunned faces. Did they think I was a pussy who was gonna deal with their shit lying down forever? Fuck that. The second Sabrina was brought into it, I wanted to rip all their heads off. "Did you and Sabrina have fun over break?" I said, reminding him of his words.

His eyes shifted back to mine and the sides of his mouth twitched.

"You messed with the wrong guy," I assured him.

"Careful." He lowered his voice so only I could hear. "You have no idea what I'm truly capable of."

I stared at him with so much ire I could taste it. I wanted to humiliate him the way he'd humiliated me. I wanted to hurt him the way he was hurting Sabrina and me. My grip tightened. If I just squeezed a little harder…

"Crosby," Xavier said from somewhere nearby.

His voice snapped me out of it. And as much as I despised Jeremy, hurting him would only give him a reason to release the video.

"Dammit," I cursed under my breath. As much as I wanted to rip him to shreds, I couldn't risk the video going viral—or me being kicked off the team.

I. Was. Fucked.

I relaxed my grip and stepped back

Jeremy groped at his throat, the red outlines of my fingers a testament to what I could've done to him. But he had me. And we both knew it.

With my emotions raging inside me, I turned to the bench holding my teammates' pads. And with one long swipe of the arm, I sent them flying all over the room. As my teammates stood frozen around the locker room, I grabbed my bag from the floor and my pads, cup, and stick from my locker and got the hell out of there.

I needed time to calm my anger—and my nerves. I wasn't one who got nervous easily, but I had a scout there to see me play. This was my shot to break out from the dark cloud my parents had brought over me. This was my chance to start over. To make money of my own so I never needed to depend on anyone else again. This was my chance to finally achieve my dream—despite assholes like Jeremy trying to stop it from happening.

I suited up in a nearby bathroom and walked out just as the team exited the locker room, following Coach to the entrance of the ice. One after another my teammates skated onto the ice. I stepped into the back of the line and skated onto the ice last.

Within seconds, alarm bells began to wail in my head.

An unfamiliar numbing sensation warmed my balls, becoming hotter as I moved around the ice. From warm to hot, heat spread out to all parts of my groin.

Oh, fuck.

Fuck, fuck, fuuuuuck.

Icy hot!!!!

In my cup.

I'd heard it was a killer, but no one ever dared to do it to me. Why would they want their star player out of commission?

But I wasn't dealing with my past teammates. I was dealing with fucked up guys like Jeremy who were jealous of my skills.

I did the only thing I could, given the current pain I was enduring. I fought the agony, circling the ice to the music blaring and lights flashing. Suddenly, everything began to blur and swirl, as if I'd taken some type of drug. My face pulsed with heat. My heart drummed faster in my chest. Sweat beaded around my hairline, down the back of my neck, then every-fucking-where. I shook my head, trying to clear the haze as I fought to push through it, but the burning became worse. The harder I skated the more it flamed. I needed to jump around. I needed to—

Fuck. Shit. Dammit.

There was no way to focus with my dick on fire. Being on plenty of teams in my life, this prank happened once a season. And the kicker was water intensified it. So even though the inclination was to jump in water, it would've made it worse.

I needed to rip off the cup. I needed to be rid of the pain.

But I needed to play.

I closed my eyes, willing the pain away, but all it did was glaze my eyes with tears. Some of my teammates watched me. Did they know what had been done to me or did I just look like I was having a panic attack?

I glanced to Sabrina who sat in the front row with Finlay, bouncing in her seat. She was so excited to be there. So excited the scout was there for me. Little did she know, my body was burning up and there was no way I'd be able to play the way I needed to in order to impress that scout.

She smiled and waved as I skated by them. I couldn't smile—for a growing number of reasons. I just skated over to the bench. The coaches spoke to each other, likely discussing last-minute changes before they relayed them to us. I knew better than to interrupt them. But the urgency of my situation trumped it.

"Coach?" I shouted over the music as my teammates continued warming up on the ice.

He turned to look at me. "What is it, Crosby?"

"I need to hit the showers."

His creased eyes conveyed his confusion. "What?"

"I need to hit the showers."

"There's a scout here to see you play and you're telling me you need a shower?"

"I'm having a problem with my—"

"Stick," Jeremy said as he skated over.

My eyes narrowed on him. "Fuck you."

"Wasn't me everyone saw you fuck," he said with a condescending grin.

"You son of a bitch." I launched myself at him, shoving him as hard as I could into the boards.

He bounced off them. "Careful, Parks," he warned as he righted himself on his skates.

"Crosby!" Coach grabbed the front of my jersey while his assistants held Jeremy back from me. "What the hell has gotten into you?"

I yanked free from him. "Ask him."

Coach glared at me. "I asked you."

My eyes shot away, my anger and pain at a breaking point.

"Scout or no scout," Coach growled. "You're not starting."

I didn't even care. I took off toward the locker room, needing to do something to ease the fucking pain, but Coach grabbed my arm. "Bench," he ordered.

At that point, tears pooled in my eyes as fire overtook my lower half. I wanted nothing more than to prove I could handle anything thrown at me, but I couldn't handle this. This was fucking torture.

I dropped down onto the bench hating that Jeremy was getting exactly what he wanted.

My chance at the pros was slipping away with every second I sat there. A sex tape was seconds away from going viral. And my dick was likely to shrivel up and fall off.

My team took the ice, and the game began. I glanced over at Sabrina who shrugged her confusion and mouthed, "Are you okay?"

I shook my head. Nothing about it was okay. My body was on fucking fire. I could barely even sit still.

A few minutes in, our opponents called a time out and Coach ordered me onto the ice. I hopped up and skated out. Every move burned like a motherfucker. Pain throbbed in my dick. A heat I'd never felt before had spread down to my legs. I could barely see through my glazed eyes as the puck dropped. I felt like I was seeing underwater. I couldn't follow the puck. I could barely hear a sound. The pain was too great. I moved around the ice, hoping the puck magically found its way to my stick. It didn't. I wasn't even in position to make a shot if it had. At some point, a whistle blew, and Coach beckoned me off the ice.

"What the hell is wrong with you?" he screamed in my face.

"Icy hot on my dick."

His eyes flared. "Jeremy?"

I shrugged, which just made him angrier.

"Go," he pointed toward the locker room. "I'll deal with you later."

I took off for the locker room, not glancing back at my team, Sabrina, or the crowd where a scout who held the key to my future sat somewhere wondering why the hell he'd even shown up.

Once I reached the locker room, I stripped down and practically ran into the showers. The water couldn't have done much worse than the pain I was feeling. If anything, the soap might've helped slightly. I scrubbed as much of the stuff off as I could, but it had absorbed itself into my skin. And even if I did feel well enough to go back out there, my cup was covered in the stuff.

"Crosby?" Sabrina called.

I stepped out of the showers with a towel wrapped around my hips, my dick still pulsing. "What are you doing in here?"

The pain in her eyes mirrored the pain in my body. "What'd they do to you?"

"Jeremy," I explained as I sat down on the wooden bench. "Put hot gel inside my cup—or at least had someone do it."

She clasped her hand over her mouth and dropped down beside me. "Are you okay?"

"I've never felt pain like this in my entire life." I lowered my head, letting my wet hair block out the sight of her beside me.

"Are you okay now? Can you go back out there?"

I shook my head. "It's too late."

"Too late? You've got a scout here to see you play."

I tunneled my fingers through my wet hair. "He probably already left."

She jumped to her feet causing me to glance up at her standing over me. Disgust shadowed her face. "So that's it? You're just giving up?"

I shrugged.

She crossed her arms with anger radiating off of her. "What's really going on, Crosby?"

"What do you mean?"

"This is your dream. You don't just give up on a dream because some jealous teammates mess with you."

I closed my eyes, unable to bear her disgust. I wanted to tell her the truth. Wanted to come clean about the video, but what the hell was I gonna say that would make it all right. Jeremy clearly had the upper hand. This stunt proved he could do whatever he wanted with no repercussions. I was damned if I ratted him out and damned if I didn't.

"So, you're not going back out there?"

I shook my head.

"You're wussing out?"

My eyes opened and locked on hers. My motives sat at the forefront of my brain, my explanation on the tip of my tongue.

"I'm not stupid Crosby. I know there's more to it than some immature hazing."

I said nothing.

"Tell me the truth," she pleaded. "Stop lying to me."

The clenching in my jaw intensified as I stared at her, knowing she was slipping away. Knowing I was *letting* her slip away.

"Talk to me, God dammit."

My heart hammered away in my chest, but the words just wouldn't leave my lips.

She stared at me, a mix of frustration, hurt, and anger marring her features.

I shrugged, which was such a feeble and spineless response. Especially, when she deserved the truth.

"That's not an answer."

"That's all I've got."

"And if that's not good enough for me?" she asked.

"Then I'm not good enough for you."

She tilted her head and shot me the same sympathetic look she gave me when she realized I'd spent Christmas alone. "That's not what I meant."

"I need you to trust me," I said, my eyes straying guiltily from hers.

"Do you trust *me*?" she asked.

"Of course."

"Then prove it. Tell me what's really going on."

I sat for a long time, wanting to talk, but so incredibly scared to.

"Is this about the draft?" she asked. "Are you worried you'll lose your chance if you talk? Because I've gotta say, what could be worse than what just happened?"

I released a long breath, the type reserved for impossible situations. "I need you to trust that I know what I'm doing."

Her subsequent silence sat so thick in the room you could've cut it with a knife. What was she thinking? What did she see when she looked at me now? A coward? A fool?

"You deserve better than me," I said, looking her straight in the eyes.

Her face scrunched. "Bullshit."

"Everything I touch goes to hell."

"I'm not gonna let you sit here and throw a pity party for yourself. You need someone who'll tell you the truth. Tell you when you're being stupid. You're being stupid."

I blinked a few times, the sting of her words much kinder than I deserved. But I didn't respond.

The silence in the room grew.

The distance between us grew.

The reality of what was happening—what I was letting happen—grew. Sabrina knew it and I knew it.

"Don't do this to me, Crosby," she said.

I said nothing as my eyes drifted away from hers.

"Don't be who I thought you were."

Her words crushed me, almost as much as the sound of her footsteps trailing out of the locker room and out of my life. And as much as it killed me to sit there and let her go, I knew she was better off without me.

CHAPTER TWENTY-ONE

Sabrina

"You need to look past your anger, Sabrina," Finlay's muffled voice carried over the music blaring through my headphones as I lay on my bed staring up at the ceiling.

It had been a week since Crosby's game. A week since I'd seen or talked to him. A week since I'd seen the cowardly side of him I despised. And as painful as that was to digest, what was worse was that he was avoiding me as much as I was avoiding him. He hadn't called, texted, or stopped by.

He wasn't fighting for me.

I don't know what I expected. Behind closed doors, he'd been so strong and determined. Why couldn't he be that guy all the time? The type who fought for me and for himself.

I removed my headphones and the country music filtered faintly into the room. "I'm allowed to be pissed."

"Of course you are. Crosby showed weakness, but not every guy can be Caden or Forester."

"Are you trying to make me feel better or worse?"

She leaned against her desk and crossed her arms. "I just want you to get over this."

"Why?"

"Because I've never seen you as happy as you were with Crosby."

"Do I look happy to you?"

Finlay cocked her head, not liking my sarcasm. "As much as you think he's hurting you, the only one he's truly hurting is himself."

"Yeah. And I'm allowed to not wanna sit by and watch it happen. Besides, it's not like he's calling me."

"Ever think there's more to it?" she asked.

Of course there was something more to it. *But he wouldn't freaking tell me.*

"Between the tree, jockstrap, and hot gel, he's put up with all of it. At some point, a guy cracks. You know him better than I do. Why hasn't he?"

"He doesn't want to make waves on the team," I said, hating how lame the excuse sounded in hindsight.

Finlay grabbed her coat from the chair and slipped it on. "Even I could only take so much of Grady before I made him think I put a laxative in his drink last year." She moved to the door and pulled it open, turning to look at me. "Maybe once you figure out what's really going on, you can go back to making those gaga eyes at Crosby."

I knew she was trying to make me feel better, but I said nothing. Because there was nothing *to* say. I walked away from him and he let me go.

Finlay's lips twisted regrettably. "I'll see you at Caden's."

I nodded, and though I wasn't in a partying mood, I owed it to her, Caden, and Forester to celebrate the football team's big championship win with them.

Finlay stepped into the hallway and closed the door behind her, leaving me alone with my thoughts.

We'd been roommates for over a year, and this was the first time she was seeing my stubbornness in full force. It was one of my greatest strengths. I'd always been someone who believed in what I thought. What I said. What I did. To hell with everyone else. But had I acted too rashly? Had I been too quick to give up on Crosby? Had I been like everyone else in his life and abandoned him when he needed me the most?

Grrrrr.

I grabbed my phone to turn off my music and a picture I'd taken of him in a towel at the hotel popped up. I hadn't removed it from my home screen yet—probably because who wouldn't want to see a hot guy every time they turned on their phone? Or maybe it was *that* hot guy I wanted to see.

Damn him for being weak.

Crosby

I suited up in the bathroom down the hall then stepped into the locker room before my next game. Every eye averted mine. I hadn't seen my teammates since the Icy Hot incident. And, since I refused to tell Coach who tampered with my cup, he hadn't allowed me to practice with the team. I think he thought I'd cave and eventually tell him, but a sex tape hanging over my head was a powerful deterrent. I knew Coach was torn—wanting to punish me for my silence, but feeling sorry that my chance with the scout got blown—because he arranged for me to have ice time alone so I could practice.

Jeremy rounded the corner and stopped short, spotting me in the locker room for the first time in a week. He stared me down, but my eyes never wavered from his. He still hadn't released the video. Xavier and I decided he was playing a mind game with me, knowing the *waiting* for it to drop would've been more torturous than the actual video being out there.

But I had news for Jeremy. Despite the video hanging over me *and* me not getting back out on the ice last game, I wouldn't let him win tonight.

Sabrina had been wrong. I wasn't the guy she once thought I was. I wouldn't be that guy again.

I'd wanted to be a pro hockey player since the first time I was fitted for skates. I had that natural ability coaches talked about when interviewed after games. Skating came easily. Scoring came easily. And body checking assholes came easily. I tasted hockey in everything I did. It was part of me and nothing Jeremy did was going to stop me from achieving my dream of playing it.

After Coach's pregame speech, I lined up in back of my teammates as they filed out of the locker room. I was eager to get onto the ice, wanting to redeem myself after the last game and curious to see if Sabrina had shown up. I'd given her front row tickets to the remainder of my games before shit hit the fan, but deep down I knew she wouldn't be there.

The lights in the arena dimmed and music echoed off the walls. I followed my teammates onto the ice, circling the perimeter of the rink like my life depended on it. But no matter how quickly I flew around the ice, it didn't make Sabrina appear in that empty seat in the front row.

Coach's whistle blew and we skated over to the bench, gathering around him holding his clipboard. As he spoke, my eyes drifted to the empty seat.

Since arriving at school, it had all been about getting through this season and making it to the pros. This had been the first time I'd put someone else before me. And what did I get to show for it? An empty seat and a broken fucking heart.

Sabrina

Music blared inside Caden and Forester's two-story house on the outskirts of campus. It was a shock the cops hadn't broken up the party already since so many people showed up to celebrate the football team's victory. By nine o'clock, the house had reached capacity, and bodies filtered outside into the front and back yards.

In my quest to find Finlay and Caden on the second floor where Caden's bedroom was, I weaved my way around familiar faces and climbed the stairs. Unfortunately, people filled the upstairs hallway creating a virtual wall. I turned back around and made my way downstairs and headed toward the kitchen.

I heard Grady's big mouth before I saw him at the kitchen table, chugging what looked like a pitcher of beer. When he slammed it back down on the table, the people around him cheered. I rolled my eyes knowing how much he loved the attention.

Somehow, he spotted me across the crowded room. "Sabrina!"

I spun around, trying to get away before he made some kind of scene. No such luck.

"Where you going?" he asked, slinging his arm over my shoulders.

"Just checking out who's here."

"Then you needn't look any further. You found me."

I shook my head as he walked me toward the living room. My entire body tensed as soon as we stepped into the crowded room. Hockey players sat around the coffee table playing a card game. My eyes shot around, searching the room for Crosby. Once I realized he wasn't there, I released the breath I'd unknowingly been holding. But just because he wasn't in the living room, didn't mean he wasn't somewhere else in the house.

Anxious butterflies filled my stomach. What would I say to him if we came face to face? Would it be uncomfortable? Difficult to make eye contact? Awkward?

"Hey, Sabrina," Jeremy called from the sofa.

My eyes narrowed on him. Why wouldn't he just go away?

"Who's that?" Grady asked, all brotherly and protective like Caden and Forester usually were.

I shook my head. "No one."

A few of the guys seated with Jeremy turned to see who he'd called to. Their eyes widened when they spotted me and they snickered. Did they know Jeremy and I had gone out? Were they amused by the disgust on my face? Or did they just think I was with Grady now?

"You wanna play flip cup in the kitchen?" Grady asked me.

I didn't, but the strange attention I was receiving from Jeremy and his friends was beginning to make me uncomfortable. Grady turned us away from them and we headed toward the kitchen, but I didn't miss the whistles and catcalls that followed us out of the room.

"Sabrina," a guy called from behind us. Over the noise, it sounded like Crosby.

I froze. Unprepared for what I'd say to him, I pulled in a deep breath and glanced over my shoulder. I relaxed when I spotted Forester squeezing his tall body through the masses to get to me.

"You missed your shot, Forester," Grady told him as he stepped in front of us. "She's all mine."

Forester patted him on the shoulder. "Got news for you, bro. She's not that easily won. She makes guys work for it." He glanced to me. "Right, Sabrina?"

"Not many guys can handle this," I said.

Forester laughed and Grady's eyes cut to mine. "Do I really have no shot?"

"No shot," I said. "But, if it helps, I'm not really looking for anything. Need a break from guys for a while."

"Finlay told me about the hockey player," Forester said.

Grady glared at me. "Hockey player? Are you kidding me? Those guys are pussies."

Forester and I laughed, but Grady looked thoroughly repulsed that I would've dated a hockey player over him.

"Do you see how many pads they wear?" he said, shaking his head in disgust. "Pussies."

It was comical coming from him. But the pit in my stomach brought on by the thought of a certain hockey player, who clearly wasn't there, just wouldn't go away. And I spent the rest of the night pretending to enjoy the party.

CHAPTER TWENTY-TWO

February

Crosby

I crossed campus with the straps of my backpack clutched in my cold hands. I had no idea February in Alabama could be so unforgiving. Across the quad, I spotted Sabrina walking beside Caden's roommate, the one they call Forester. It had been two weeks since she walked out of my life, and it took everything in me not to quicken my pace and approach her. Instead, I watched from a safe distance. A cold knot formed in the deep recesses of my gut at the way her smile beamed when she spoke to him. At one time that smile had been reserved for me.

I stopped walking and watched as Forester placed his hand on her head and messed up her hair like a big brother would do to his sister. Maybe she wasn't moving on with him, but she would move on. I'd given her no reason not to. And if that video ever went viral, she'd do more than move on.

Xavier had been keeping an eye out for it, and it still wasn't out there. I'd be lying if I said it wasn't torture waiting for it to be released. I was constantly wondering what Jeremy was waiting for. What I'd do to push him to do it. Maybe he already had the time planned out. Who the hell knew…

Sabrina hurried away from Forester and climbed the steps to the psych building.

Images of our time there over Christmas break plagued my mind. All the nights I'd snuck her in. All the times she'd kept me company…and busy. Now the building was nothing but a reminder of how much my life sucked.

Sabrina

I rushed inside the building and ducked around the corner, leaning against the wall and dragging in deep breaths. It hadn't been easy to avoid Crosby the way I had been. I didn't realize how many times our paths would've crossed over the course of a day if I hadn't taken up new routes to classes and found different places to eat.

My phone vibrated in my pocket. I slipped it out and lifted it to my ear. "Hey, Mom. How was the cruise?"

"Oh, my goodness. It was so nice and relaxing. But we missed you."

"I know. School always gets in the way. I should just quit and travel the world with you guys."

"Bite your tongue," she admonished.

I laughed.

"So, how's the new semester going?"

I glanced around at the students rushing in and out of the building before I turned to face the wall to obstruct the noise. "It's fine."

"Fine's not amazing," my mother said. "How's Crosby?"

Why was Crosby the only thing anyone wanted to talk about? "I'm not sure. We're not seeing each other anymore."

"What happened?"

"I really don't feel like talking about it."

"Oh, honey." There was a long pause on her end. I knew what came next. And I really didn't want to be lectured. "If love was easy, there wouldn't be so many divorces."

"Mom, I just met the guy. I wasn't thinking about marriage."

"I know that. It was an analogy. You need to graduate and find a job before you consider settling down with someone."

"Actually…finding a job might take longer than I initially thought."

"Why?" I could hear the fear in her voice. "Are you failing a class?"

"No. But I think I might wanna go to law school."

A deafening silence filled her end.

"Okay, you can pick your jaw up off the floor now. I know it sounds crazy, but I think I can do it."

"Of course, you can do it," she said, sounding surer than even I was. "I'm just surprised, that's all. You never mentioned you were interested in law."

"I know. But I think I've got what it takes."

"There's not a doubt in my mind you'll make an amazing lawyer." I could hear the pride in her voice. "You're determined and strong and you care about other people. Hold on, I want you to tell your dad the big news."

"Tell your dad what?" my dad said, getting on the phone.

"Hey, Dad."

"What's your big news?"

"I'm thinking of declaring a major in pre-law. Then going to law school."

"No way?"

I laughed. "Yup. Your daughter's gonna be a lawyer."

"Thank God. I was wondering how you were gonna take care of us when we got old."

"Easy buddy. I could still put you in a home."

His laughter rumbled through the phone. "So, no engagement to that hockey player then?" I knew his little girl's happiness was his top priority, so I almost felt bad admitting my relationship with Crosby had failed.

"No. We're not seeing each other anymore."

His laughter quickly disappeared and his protective side took over. "He hurt you?"

I pulled in a frustrated breath. "No. He let some people hurt *him* and did nothing to fight back. You always taught me not to be a punching bag. And for some reason Crosby is."

"That's his choice," my dad reminded me.

"Yeah, and it's my choice not to stick around to see it happen."

"Did you ask him why he's doing it?"

"I thought I knew. But now I have no idea."

"You think his family issues have something to do with it?"

"I have no idea. I never wanted to pry." I guess I didn't know Crosby as well as I thought I did. I only knew what he wanted me to know. And a relationship couldn't work like that. He made sure of it.

"Well, go easy on him," my dad said. "He's had it tough."

"Yeah." Crosby *had* had it tough. There was no denying that.

"Ever wonder why people want to hurt him?" my dad asked.

My dad's words stilled me.

He was right.

I'd been so focused on why Crosby didn't fight back. Maybe a better question would have been why wouldn't Jeremy leave him alone?

CHAPTER TWENTY-THREE

Crosby

I tipped back my bottle of beer, watching the hockey game on the wide-screen in the bar. Chekhov, a five-time pro all-star, took off with the puck, dodging his opponents effortlessly on the screen. Unfortunately, the noise mixed with the music in the crowded bar made it impossible to hear the commentators calling the game.

"He's a beast," Xavier said from the stool beside me. "Who knows, bro, after your two goals tonight, you could be playing beside him next year."

I may have scored a couple goals, but that didn't matter if the people who mattered most weren't there to see them. A tap on my shoulder had my head whipping over my shoulder.

A brunette from my history class stood there, her low-cut shirt leaving little to the imagination. "Hi there."

"Hey."

She slipped onto the empty stool on my right and spun to face me. "Who you here with?"

I ticked my head to the side. "Xavier."

"Hey," Xavier said, leaning forward so she could see him on the opposite side of me.

She gave him a cursory look before her eyes jumped back to me. "I love your ink." Her hand landed on my bicep and drifted over my arm. "I've got a couple, too. Wanna know where?"

I lifted my bottle to my lips and finished the rest of my beer.

"If he doesn't wanna know," Xavier said. "I assure you, I do."

She huffed, obviously not getting the attention from me she hoped for. "Heard you scored tonight," she said, seemingly taking a different approach.

I nodded.

"Twice," Xavier added.

Her eyes never left mine. "If we take it back to my place, you might be able to make it three times."

Xavier choked on the other side of me.

"Sorry," I said to her. "I'm sure you're a great girl, but I'm just chillin' with Xavier tonight." With that, I focused back on the hockey game on the TV. I watched intently until I felt her leave my side.

"Dude," Xavier said.

I looked to him.

"You're either a rock star or a complete idiot."

I laughed.

"The girl invited you home with her and you sent her packing."

"I wasn't interested."

He snorted, his eyes searching the bar for wherever she'd disappeared to. "Who wouldn't be interested in that?"

In the past, I assumed girls hit on me because I played hockey and had an impressive body. But now my father's words played in my mind. And I hated the fact that anything he said stuck with me. But had he been right about girls' motives? Would I ever really know why someone was with me?

Someone tapped my shoulder and my body tensed. I was in no mood to deal with any more drunk girls. I turned slowly.

"I thought that was you," Caden said, standing there with his hands in his pockets.

Instinctively, I checked to see if the girls were with him.

"Sabrina's not here."

I nodded, realizing how obvious I'd made it. "How she doing?"

He shrugged. "Haven't seen her. Finlay said she's been disappearing a lot lately."

"She seeing someone?" I asked, trying for nonchalance, though my gut clenched at the thought of it.

"Not that I know of. But listen," his voice lowered, conspiratorially. "Finlay wanted me to come over here and check things out. You know, so she could report back to Sabrina."

"Sabrina cut me loose," I reminded him.

He chuckled. "I gave up trying to figure out girls a long time ago."

Xavier held out his fist to Caden. "Congrats, man. Great game against Georgia."

Caden bumped his fist. "Thanks." His eyes jumped back to mine. "So, I can tell her you're not seeing anyone?"

I nodded.

"Okay," Caden said, looking to the TV as Chekhov shot and scored his second goal of the night. "I'll let you guys get back to your game."

"Later," I said.

"Later," Xavier called.

I glanced over my shoulder as Caden returned to the table with Finlay. She eagerly listened to what I assumed was Caden's "report" before glancing over at me. I lifted my empty beer bottle in acknowledgment.

She smiled and lifted hers.

Sabrina

It was quiet on the third floor in the library as I slunk back in my chair surrounded by dusty scholarly journals most undergrads had no use for. For the third day in a row, I'd been tucked away at a back table. My eyes burned and I'd begun to question if I knew what I was even looking for.

My phone vibrated. I searched for it beneath the papers strewn across the table. I located it and found a text from Finlay. **Where are you?**

My thumbs pounded away at my screen. **Library. Third floor.**

On my way. Saw Crosby at the bar last nite. Need to talk to you.

A shudder rushed through me. What did she need to talk to me about? Was Crosby alright? Had she talked to him? Had he moved on?

A few minutes later I looked up to find Finlay standing there, her eyes moving over the articles covering the table.

"What are you doing?" she asked.

"I did what you said." I grabbed a handful of papers and straightened them into a pile. "I looked past my anger."

Confusion flashed across her face. "So, you're burying yourself in schoolwork?"

"Not quite."

Finlay slipped into the chair across from me. "What's that mean?"

I didn't know how to respond. I hadn't really found anything substantial. "What did you need to tell me about Crosby?"

"Some girl was trying to get his attention. Touching his tattoos and stuff."

I grabbed more loose papers and neatened them into another pile, trying to remain unfazed by the unwanted image flashing in my mind. "So?"

"So, I had Caden go check things out."

"Why? Crosby can do what he wants."

She pegged me with her eyes. "He's not seeing anyone, if you were wondering."

I handed her a stack of papers, a small sense of relief spreading over me.

She flipped through them, looking them over curiously. "Why are these names highlighted?"

"They're the people suing Crosby's parents."

"There are hundreds of them."

I nodded.

She looked at me. "Why are you interested in who's suing Crosby's parents?"

"I'm looking for familiar names. Names that might tell me why he thinks he has to put up with what's been happening to him."

"Have you found anything yet?"

I shook my head. "No names stood out, so I started researching each of them. I'm not even halfway through the list yet."

She stared across the table at me. "Sabrina."

I met her gaze, hating the pity in her eyes.

"You should've told me. I would've helped you."

I handed her a pile. "Then what are you waiting for? Get searching."

She smiled.

"I've got more printouts," Grady said, approaching the table with the stack of papers he'd fetched from the copy machine.

Finlay stared at him. "*He's* helping you?"

"*He* has a name," Grady said, tossing the papers down in front of me and sliding into the seat beside Finlay.

I laughed as he wrapped his arm around her shoulders. She jumped out of the seat and circled the table to sit beside me, avoiding Grady at all costs.

But regardless of their love-hate relationship, the three of us didn't leave that table for the next five hours until we found what we were looking for.

CHAPTER TWENTY-FOUR

Sabrina

I leaned against the outside of the campus gym, impatience overwhelming me. The door opened and closed, people in workout clothes coming and going all day.

After what felt like hours, the door opened and one of Crosby's teammates came out. He was a tall guy with long strides, so I hurried to catch up as he walked away. "Mathews, right?"

He looked to me, his dark eyes widening like he knew me. "Yeah?"

"Question for you. What'd Jeremy Potter do to get you to tie Crosby to that tree?"

Guilt crossed his face. "Who said I did that?"

"You want the list?"

His pace quickened and I struggled to keep up with him. "So, what if I did?"

"Just wondering what he had on you to make you do it?"

"Who said I didn't want to help?"

I grasped hold of his arm and stopped him. "Come on. The guy's an asshole."

He looked away from me, somewhere over my shoulder. "What's it matter to you?" he asked.

"I dated Jeremy," I explained, though his eyes hadn't returned to me yet. "Not one of my proudest moments."

"Hey, Mathews" a stocky guy I also recognized from the hockey team said, stepping up beside us. He looked at me, unapologetically assessing me, particularly my boobs. "The video definitely didn't do you justice."

Mathews, looking guilty as ever, shoved him. "Shut up."

Fear spread over me. "What video?"

"See ya," the guy said, taking off before I could stop him.

I grabbed Mathews' arm again. "Talk."

"You're not gonna like this."

"Talk!"

People around us paused, watching what appeared to be a lovers' quarrel.

"There's a video of you and Parks."

My heart ricocheted off the wall of my chest. "What kind of video?"

He nodded, the only explanation necessary.

"Who?" I demanded as a cold sweat began to spread over me.

"Who do you think?"

"Say it!"

"Jeremy."

"Show it to me," I demanded.

My heart sank as he slipped out his phone. I wanted him to say he didn't have it, but he pulled it up on his screen as if he had it saved to his favorites. And just like that Crosby and I were going at it in the library one of the nights I kept him company at work. My shirt was off and little remained to the imagination. As soon as I heard myself moan, I stopped the video and forwarded it to myself. "Is this online?"

He shook his head. "Not yet. I think only the hockey team's seen it."

Images of the party and the strange looks they gave me came rushing back at me. "Has Crosby?"

He paused.

A million thoughts whirled through my mind while I watched him contemplate his response.

He nodded slowly.

Crosby's words played in my head. *You deserve better than me…Everything I touch goes to hell.* He knew. And he was trying to tell me—or at least trying to push me away. Was he trying to protect me?

I shoved the phone back at Mathews. "You need to delete that or I'll go to the dean. Nonconsensual recordings are illegal. And as far as the dean knows, the one who has it is the one who recorded it."

I spun away from him and sped across campus with a knot swelling in my throat making it difficult to swallow.

What I'd seen on that video.

What I'd heard.

God.

If it was released, how could I stay on campus? How could I get into law school? A sex tape would follow me for the rest of my life.

My phone buzzed in my pocket, jolting my already jumpy body. I slipped it out and a text from Finlay sat on my screen. **He's in the dining hall.**

I quickened my pace, trudging across campus. My scalp felt as though it was about to split in two as the cool breeze whipped my hair around my face. But it didn't stop me—or ease the heat pulsing in my cheeks.

I entered the crowded dining hall, stopping at Finlay and Caden's table.

"How'd it go?" Finlay asked as I dropped into the seat beside her, needing a moment to process everything I'd seen.

I didn't look at her or Caden, too numb to speak. I looked around the busy room. My eyes stopped, zoning in on Jeremy seated across the way with some of his teammates. My heartbeat thumped in my temples, cloaking all the sounds in that noisy room.

I sprang to my feet.

"Whoa." Finlay grasped my wrist. "What are you gonna do?"

"Take down the asshole."

She dropped my wrist, knowing enough to let me do what I needed to do.

The sight of Jeremy laughing with his friends had pushed me over the edge. I strode across the room, weaving around crowded tables as my heartbeat pulsed in tandem with my steps. I stopped at Jeremy's table.

Sensing me hovering over him, he looked up.

"Can I talk to you, Jeremy?" I asked, fighting the urge to jump across the table and claw out his eyeballs.

"You're talking," he said, all snide and pompous.

Some of his friends snickered.

"I guess I am," I said, feigning ignorance while wanting nothing more than to hurt him the way he'd hurt Crosby and me.

He looked purposefully around the room. "Where's your boyfriend?"

"He's not my boyfriend."

Jeremy snorted. "A girl like you gets around then, huh?"

Again, his friends snickered.

I looked each of them dead in the eyes and smiled. "Laugh again and I'll kick you so hard in the balls you'll be limping for the foreseeable future."

Their faces sobered.

My focus returned to Jeremy. "I think you misunderstood me, so I'll say it again. I need to talk to you."

He huffed in annoyance. "You've got three minutes." He pushed back his chair and stood.

"It'll only take two." *Asshole.*

We weaved our way around the tables until we stepped outside. Jeremy stopped by the short brick wall in front of the building and sat on it, his arms crossed as if already bored with our conversation. "Speak."

"I know I was a pawn in this vendetta you've got against Crosby."

"Did he tell you that?"

"He didn't have to. It was clear when you asked me out. Then again when you grilled me about my meeting with the dean. Then again when you sent me to Crosby's room instead of yours. Should I keep going because the list seems to be growing by the hour?"

His eyes drifted to the students moving around campus. "Did he send you here?"

"Why would he send me here?"

"To get me to back off."

"Back off?" I cocked my head. "You admitting to something?"

He scoffed as his eyes followed a pretty girl who passed by us.

"Your bracelet said, 'Potters never give up.' Is this what it looks like? Is this what your parents would want?"

His eyes flew back to mine, darkness flashing in his expression. "What did you say?"

"I know Crosby's parents hurt your family."

His stare narrowed coldly. "So, he does know?"

I shook my head. "I don't think he does. But it's online for anyone who bothers to look. I didn't catch it at first. Your last name isn't the same as your father's."

"What do you want?"

"The better question is what do *you* want? It wasn't Crosby who hurt you. You get that, right? It was his parents and they're both in jail."

"They took everything from us."

"So, you're gonna destroy *Crosby's* future?"

"Why not?"

"What about mine?"

His brows climbed. "Yours?"

"I know about the video."

He said nothing, but the vindictiveness in his eyes and the subtle grin tugging up the sides of his mouth said it all. He had no remorse.

I glared back at him, disgusted by the mere sight. "Did you get off watching us together, you sick bastard?"

He rolled his eyes.

"You jealous he got what you didn't?" I kept pushing, hoping he'd snap and reveal what he'd done.

He scoffed.

"You act like you don't care, but it's one more thing he took from you. And we both know he's better than you at hockey."

"He's not better than me," he said.

"I've seen him play. He's headed for the pros. You know it and I know it."

"Not if I have anything to do with it," he murmured.

"You've already had something to do with it. You wrecked his chances with the scout," I said.

"You've got no proof of that."

"You're right. But I do have proof you tied him to that tree."

"Sure you do."

"Your teammates aren't as loyal as you think. How do you think I know about the video?"

Anger brewed in his eyes.

"Karma's a bitch, Potter. And so am I." With that I spun away and took off, knowing he was shooting daggers at me with his eyes. I lifted my hand into the air and flipped him off.

CHAPTER TWENTY-FIVE

Sabrina

Dean Edwards and I stared at each other across his desk. It was the first time I'd been back since the tree incident. So much had happened since then. And as I sat there, with my phone in my hand, I wished I'd told him what I'd known right from the beginning. It would have saved us all a lot of unnecessary trouble.

I placed my phone on the dean's desk, turning up the volume to be sure he didn't miss a word. Mathews' voice filled the office, our earlier conversation recorded specifically for the dean.

Dean Edwards sat there, watching my phone.

The audio switched to Jeremy's voice and our conversation outside the dining hall played. Every word a near confession of his guilt. Sure, it would never be permitted in a court of law, but it had to be enough concrete evidence for the dean to finally hand out a punishment to the right person.

Dean Edwards stared at my phone, even after it stopped playing.

"Obviously, I have the video," I said, knowing I'd fight tooth and nail to stop from having to show it to him. "And I'm sure Mathews will confirm his involvement if you call him in."

He shook his head, outwardly disgusted by what he'd heard. "I've heard enough."

"Jeremy's been putting Crosby through hell since he got here," I continued. "And even though Crosby won't talk, I don't believe Jeremy deserves to get away with it. No matter what issues he has with Crosby's family."

Dean Edwards pressed a button on his phone and his secretary answered. "Find the phone numbers for Jeremy Potter's parents. I need them to come to campus immediately."

"And if they ask what this is about?" his secretary asked over the speaker.

"Tell them their boy is fine, but that this is an urgent matter." He disconnected that call and pressed another button. Campus security answered.

"I going to need two officers sent to pick up Jeremy Potter."

Relief washed over me. Crosby may not have wanted to take Jeremy down for fear of the repercussions, but I felt damn good knowing the asshole was about to get what he had coming.

The dean hung up the phone. With a deep exhalation, he looked to me sadly. "All I ever wanted was for this university to be a safe place for students. I hope you don't think I was too harsh last time you were here. I was just following protocol and trying to get to the truth so I could punish whoever tried to hurt Crosby."

"I understand that now."

He nodded. "Crosby's here because of me. His mother and I were classmates. So, when she contacted me about the potential problems facing Crosby if he stayed in Texas, I allowed him to enroll here. I promised her I'd take care of him."

"And the first thing that happened when he arrived was he got hazed," I said, finishing his thought for him.

"Exactly. Not only had I let *him* down by not giving him the safe place his mother sought for him, but I let *her* down."

"Crosby's okay. He's a lot stronger than people think. *And*, he's got me looking out for him."

A sad smile tipped his lips. "He's lucky to have you. I'm sorry I couldn't have helped sooner."

Crosby

The puck flew across the ice. I waited to the left of the goal and stopped it with ease, firing it at our goal. Our goalie nearly got his glove on it, but it sailed past him. Coach blew his whistle, signaling a change of drill. I stopped where I stood, waiting for Coach to tell us where to be. He'd finally allowed me back to practice, but he kept Jeremy and me apart at all times. He clearly knew something had happened between us, even if I didn't blame the cup stunt on him.

A door slammed and two campus cops entered the arena, their steps determined and echoing off the rink walls. Everyone on the ice turned, watching them approach our assistant coach, the closest one to them. They said something to him before he signaled Coach over.

With rapt attention, we watched their interaction with Coach. The cops did all the talking. Coach listened and then reached into his pocket, pulling out his phone. His thumbs pounded away at the screen before he lifted it to his ear. He listened to whoever he'd called while pacing up and down the bench area for a good three minutes. As he did, the color drained from his face. Anger brimmed in his eyes. And his steps became louder. He made a few comments into the phone then listened some more. After another few minutes, he disconnected the call and jammed his phone into his pocket.

He stared off into space for what felt like an eternity, pondering whatever he'd just heard.

His eyes eventually moved to the ice, moving slowly over every one of us, his mind clearly plagued by something. "Jeremy," he called.

Jeremy looked around confused, before skating over to him.

We remained motionless as Coach spoke to him.

Whatever he said sobered Jeremy's features. Coach shook his head as Jeremy protested. Given the anger in Coach's eyes, he wasn't hearing it. Jeremy yanked his practice jersey over his head and threw it into Coach's chest, before skating off the ice.

The cops met him at the door of the rink and followed him to the locker room.

What the hell just happened? I met Xavier's eyes on the opposite side of the rink. He shrugged his confusion. I glanced around at all of Jeremy's friends. They looked like they wanted to crawl into holes and disappear.

I looked back to Coach. He spoke to his assistant, his hands tunneling through his hair. After a few minutes, he blew his whistle and gestured for us to come over. We skated to the bench, gathering around him. "I know how rumors spread and I want you to have the truth from me before you hear lies from anyone else. Jeremy is no longer a student here."

My teammates exchanged nervous looks, all of them too scared to say a word.

Coach pegged each of them with his eyes. "Hazing is against university policy—whether you're the one doing it or a witness who doesn't try to stop it. Either way, it will no longer be tolerated on this team."

My teammates lowered their heads like the guilty cowards they were.

"Xavier will be taking Jeremy's spot in tomorrow night's game," Coach said.

Xavier didn't even bother hiding his excitement, punching his fist into the air. I didn't have to wonder. I knew it was a combination of him getting a starting position *and* Jeremy going down.

"Now, I want you all back out there running drills," Coach said. "Crosby, I need you for a minute."

All the others skated off with our assistant who fired off directions at them. Xavier beamed as he skated out to his new position.

Once they began their drill, Coach turned to me. "I reported the cup incident to the dean."

My face dropped. "How'd you know who did it?"

He cocked his head. "He was the one you slammed into the boards."

I scoffed.

"But since I didn't have proof it was him, the dean was hesitant to expel him."

"So, what changed?"

"He received evidence of Jeremy's motives."

"Jeremy's motives? Coach, I'm not following."

"He just met with Jeremy's lawyer and parents. Somehow, they were able to secure a deal that would keep him out of jail. He's about to find out now."

"No one hates the guy more than me, but could he really go to jail for hazing?"

"This was more than hazing, Crosby. He was trying to destroy your life the way your parents destroyed his family's."

My eyes couldn't have stretched any wider. "What?"

"You didn't know?"

I shook my head, a hundred thoughts swirling through my head at once.

It hadn't been hazing.

It hadn't been jealousy.

It had been payback.

Payback for what my parents had done.

How had I not seen it?

"You've got nothing to worry about now," Coach assured me.

But that was the last thing I heard before I saw red. I took off like a madman toward the locker room. I rounded the corner and somehow, even with my skates and pads on, I flew across the room, shoving Jeremy into the lockers behind him and leveling him with a right hook to the face.

The cops who stood nearby lunged forward.

"That was your one free shot," one of the cops said as he pulled me off Jeremy.

The other grabbed hold of Jeremy who bent over clutching his cheek.

With my chest rising and falling and adrenaline rushing through me, I glared at Jeremy. "You're lucky they're here. You're lucky I didn't kill you for what you did to me. What you did to Sabrina."

"What about me?" Jeremy asked, spitting a wad of blood on the floor.

"You?" I blinked furiously. "I did *nothing* to you."

He stared at me with a red cheek and swelling eye.

I hated that my parents hurt other people—and under other circumstances, I might've felt bad for Jeremy, but it didn't mean I deserved to be hurt anymore because of them. "You need help," I said. "Get it. And then you'll see we both got fucked over because of my father. It wasn't only you he hurt."

"Are you good?" the cop holding me asked. "I need to get him out of here."

"Yeah," I said.

He released me and helped his partner escort Jeremy, with his head hanging down, out of the locker room.

I dropped onto the bench, the last few minutes proving too much for me to even fully process.

Coach burst into the locker room, searching the now empty space.

"He's gone," I said.

"Did you hit him?"

"Yup."

"Feel better?"

I shrugged, having no fucking clue what I felt. I was still reeling from the information. Still pissed the fuck off. Still scared to allow myself to believe it was over.

"The dean wants you to file a restraining order, but now I'm wondering if Jeremy will be taking one out on you." Nervous laughter followed his words.

I didn't bother looking up at him as I unlaced my skates that suddenly felt too tight.

"Once you file it, he won't be allowed to contact you," Coach assured me. "If he does, the authorities will be called and he'll be facing serious repercussions."

I said nothing, my mind still struggling to make sense of everything he was saying. Everything that had happened to me. Everything that happened to Sabrina because of me.

"Do you understand what I'm telling you?" Coach asked, likely noticing the dazed expression on my face.

I nodded.

"I wish you would've talked to me," he said.

My eyes finally lifted to his, still stunned Jeremy's vendetta against me ran so deep. "He had me by the balls, Coach."

He shook his head, clearly disgusted by the turn of events. "You're lucky to have such a determined girl."

My forehead wrinkled. "What?"

"Your girlfriend. She's the one who brought the proof to the dean."

My head fell back and a delirious laugh escaped me. I'd underestimated what a stubborn and determined girl Sabrina was. She didn't get the information she wanted from me, so she found it out for herself.

All the emotions I'd been holding back since she'd shut me out flooded my body. She did care. She did have my back.

Coach stood. "Okay. I've gotta confiscate all the guys' phones now."

My brows inverted.

"Apparently, the dean has an IT guy waiting at his office to rid them of any potentially harmful videos."

It was as if a giant boulder had been lifted off not only my shoulders but my entire body. No one else would see that video. And no one else could share it. Sabrina would remain unscathed.

Coach walked to the exit, turning back as if he'd forgotten something. "Oh. And Crosby. I'm gonna have to get that scout back out here to see you play."

I closed my eyes for a moment and relief filled my body. This thing was finally over. My life could proceed. And I might just get the ending I'd been hoping for. "I won't let you down this time," I assured Coach.

"I know, kid."

CHAPTER TWENTY-SIX

Crosby

Except for the scattered lights inside Sabrina's dorm, I stood in darkness. "Tighter," I said.

"Seriously?" Xavier asked from behind the tree where he knotted the ropes that bound me to it.

"Yup."

He complied, pulling them even tighter. "So, you want me to go up there or text her?"

"Text her. That way you don't come down together."

"Got it," he said.

"You just about done?" I asked, craning my neck to see.

"I think so. You can't move, right?"

I could barely wiggle my arms that were pinned to my sides. Luckily, my Henley protected them from the unforgiving fibers of the rope. Learned that one the hard way. "Nope."

"Okay." He stepped around the tree and stood in front of me. "You sure about this?"

"Nope. But I'm here."

"Yes, you are," he chuckled, pulling my phone from my pocket and texting Sabrina. "Okay. It's sent. Now let's hope she comes down." He tucked my phone back in my pocket. "Good luck."

"Thanks."

"You want me to stay in case things go wrong?"

I shook my head. "I'll be fine."

He sent me one last smile before turning and hurrying down the path to his dorm.

I watched the front door of Sabrina's dorm, anxious to see her yet nervous for her reaction. The cool air gave me the bolt of energy I needed for the impending conversation.

Minutes passed.

No one came or went.

Finally, the front door swung open and Sabrina stepped outside in a T-shirt and jeans. The sight of her hurt my heart. She squinted into the darkness, assessing everything from the cars parked in front of her dorm to the people heading home to their dorms from their six o'clock classes.

I stood silently, waiting for her to see me. She didn't.

"Hey," I called.

Her head whipped around, but still, she didn't notice me.

"Over here."

She spun in the opposite direction, searching the darkness until she finally spotted me. She froze, staring wide-eyed at me tied to the big tree in front of her dorm. "Are you okay?" she called.

I smiled, which clearly alleviated any concern she might've had that I got myself tied to a tree for a second time. "You gonna help me or what?"

Her movements were slow, her steps almost strategic in their poise. "I'm having a strange case of déjà vu."

"Tell me about it."

"What did you do?" she asked, finally stepping in front of me and assessing the ropes.

"What did *you* do?"

She shrugged, though she had to realize the magnitude of what she'd done for me.

"I don't even know how to thank you."

"So, you tied yourself to a tree?" she asked.

"I wanted us to start over. Thought it was a good place to start."

Her eyes dropped to the ground, and she remained silent for a long time, so long I wondered if she'd leave me there. Her eyes finally lifted to mine. "I'm so sorry."

"*You're* sorry? For what?"

"For avoiding you. For getting mad about you not putting up a fight. For not trusting that you knew what you were doing."

"There was a video," I admitted.

"I know."

"You know?"

She nodded solemnly.

"I'm so damn sorry you were brought into my mess."

Anger flashed in her eyes. "You have nothing to be sorry about. I hate Jeremy for what he did to you. What he did to *us*."

"I thought I could stop him from sharing it so you never even had to know about it. I thought I could handle it alone."

A sad smile graced her lips. "You did handle it alone. Now you've got me."

Her honesty nearly did me in. "Do I?"

She crossed her arms and laid on the sass. "Well, do you plan on making it to the pros or are you gonna let some other psychopath get in your way?"

I stifled a smile. "You saying you only want me if I'm gonna be rich some day?"

She smirked. "It certainly doesn't hurt." She circled the tree to see the situation I'd put myself in. "These are some big knots," she called from behind the tree. "Who'd you piss off to get yourself in this situation?"

"This girl who meant a lot to me."

"She *meant* a lot? She doesn't anymore?"

"No. She means everything," I admitted.

She was quiet for a moment, and I would've given anything to see her reaction to my words. "You should be naked," she finally said. "Seems only right."

I laughed. "I'm hoping that happens after you untie me."

"Is that right?"

"Uh, huh."

She stepped around the tree until she stood in front of me, our toes nearly touching. She pressed her hands to my chest and dropped her forehead to mine, her familiar scent seeping into my pores for the first time in weeks. The warmth of her body and the gentleness of her touch felt like home. "This is the most messed up thing a guy has ever done for me."

"Protecting you from a sex tape or tying himself to a tree?"

She laughed, and I relished in the sound of it.

"I missed you so damn much," I said.

She lifted her warm hands to my cheeks. Had my arms not been bound to my sides, I would've wrapped them around her and never let her go again. She leaned forward and kissed me. Her lips were a self-propelled force to be reckoned with and I didn't mind one damn bit she was in charge. She kissed me like she meant it. Like she missed the taste of me. Like she'd forgiven me.

She eventually pulled away and enlisted the help of some people passing by to untie me. The second I could touch her, I lifted her off her feet and carried her over my shoulder toward her room. She didn't fight it. She just laughed. We passed plenty of people on our way upstairs. They all smiled or laughed, but none of them understood how right it felt to have her forgiveness or to have her back in my arms.

And for the first time in a long time, I knew everything was gonna be okay.

Sabrina

Inside my room, Crosby slammed the door shut and placed me up against it. His lips crashed down on mine, his tongue diving inside my mouth, holding me prisoner. This wasn't a kiss of forgiveness, this was him wanting to own every part of me, and me allowing him to do it right there and then.

His hands burrowed into my hair and he pulled back to look at me, all breathless and turned on. "You will never avoid me again."

I nodded, locked in on the intensity in his eyes.

He leaned forward and buried his lips in my neck, nipping at my skin with his teeth, harder than ever before. "You will never again see me put up with anyone's shit."

My head dropped back against the door and I closed my eyes, loving his commanding tone of voice and the assurance of his words.

He trailed open-mouthed kisses over my collarbone. "You will know that whatever I'm doing has a reason and I'm nobody's bitch." His deep voice rumbled against my chest, spreading everywhere. "And you will never, *ever*, let another guy fuck you the way I'm about to."

Tremors charged through my body, and the anticipation of what he'd do to me sent a wave of lightheadedness over me.

He pulled back so we saw nothing but each other. "Now I've got one question for you."

"What?" I breathed.

"Will you let me love you?"

I froze, my wide eyes still locked on his.

"Are you gonna let me do that?" he asked, the sudden vulnerability in his eyes all-encompassing.

With my body on the verge of imploding if he didn't bring me to my bed, I nodded.

His smile would've brought me to my knees had he not been holding onto me. He leaned in and kissed me, stealing my breath away. Then, he carried me to my bed and tossed me down like I weighed nothing at all.

I scooted back, yanking off my T-shirt and leaning back on my elbows. He pulled off his Henley and crawled on top of me, lowering me onto my back. He dropped his head and placed open-mouthed kisses over my chest. My desperation for his touch intensified with every breath. But Crosby was taking his time. Taunting me. Driving me mad.

"I appreciate the fact that you're taking your time with me," I said. "But right now is not the time."

He lifted his head with a smirk on his face. "Is that so?"

I nodded.

He reached behind my back and unsnapped my bra, tugging it off my arms and tossing it behind him. He dipped his head and sucked my nipple into his mouth. I gasped and my head dropped back against the pillow and my hands grasped onto his arms, desperately missing the feel of them around me.

For the remainder of the night, Crosby ravaged my body, exacting the punishment I deserved for abandoning him and doubting he knew what he was doing. For not realizing he was only trying to protect me and my future. For not seeing he was exactly who I needed from day one.

I swore to myself, from that night forward, I would never underestimate him *ever* again.

EPILOGUE

Three Years Later

Sabrina

I flew out of my seat and banged on the glass in front of me. A player from the opposing team had Crosby in a headlock mere feet away on the ice, punching at his chest with his oversized gloves. From what Crosby told me, with all the pads they wore, they couldn't feel a thing—unless the helmets and gloves came off. Then, it was no holds barred.

The fans around me jumped to their feet, screaming and cheering like the wild hockey fanatics I'd come to know and love. If I'd learned anything from Crosby's time in the pros, hockey fans lived for the sport—and the fights.

I watched Crosby relent and let his opponent punch him. What was he doing?

That's when it hit me.

That fool.

As soon as the crowd got into it, he slipped out of the headlock and dropped his gloves, going at his opponent with everything he had.

Eventually, the refs intervened, making a big show of pulling them apart. As Crosby was pushed by me toward the penalty box, I caught him wink beneath his helmet.

I shook my head, still loving his cocky ways.

After the game, I remained in my seat as the rest of the arena cleared out. I placed my normal post-game calls to Finlay and Caden to brag about Crosby's two goals and to Crosby's mom to give her the opportunity to do the same to me. Even though she'd won her appeal and been released from prison a few months earlier, she was required to remain in Texas. I knew she would've given anything to be there for her son. But watching him on television and getting her nightly calls made her just as happy.

I tucked my phone into my bag. Workers swept up spilled popcorn and picked up empty beer cups, paying me no notice in my front spot. They were used to me. No one but me occupied that seat. And even though the other girlfriends and wives sat in the boxes up above, Crosby wanted me where he could see me. And even after all these years, I liked knowing he did.

"Whatcha thinking about?"

My smile sprang free knowing who I'd find when I turned my head. "You."

Crosby approached with a grin, his wet hair slicked back and his cheeks still flushed from his workout on the ice. He wore a white sleeveless shirt, though he held the button-down and tie required before and after games. He stopped once he stood in front of me, leaning down and kissing me.

"Keep it PG, Parks," I smiled as he pulled back.

"When we get home, we're going right to X."

I laughed, loving that I was the one who got to go home with him every night—at least the nights he was home. Away games were lonely, but with law school filling most of my hours, it worked for us.

"How'd I look out there?"

"Same as usual. Amazing."

He laughed as he slipped his arm into his button-down shirt. The tattoo on his left bicep caught my attention as it normally did.

"Show me," I said, just as giddy as the first time I'd seen it.

A cocky smile tipped his lips. "Show you what?"

"You know."

He laughed as he twisted his arm so I could see the vibrant ink of a golden crown with the word *ice* interlocked in it on his bicep.

"That's my favorite."

"Mine too. Now show *me*," he said, the authority in his voice a total turn-on.

I twisted in my seat and lifted my *Parks* jersey so he could see my hip. Two small crisscrossed hockey sticks with *Parks* on the handles graced the area.

He shook his head. "Not that."

I laughed to myself as I dropped the hem of the jersey and held out my left hand. My engagement ring sparkled in the bright arena lights.

He grabbed hold of my hand. "I can't wait to make you Mrs. Parks."

"I can't wait to be Mrs. Parks."

He pulled me to my feet and wrapped his arms around me, burying his nose below my ear. "I can't wait to give you lots of babies."

"You're just gonna give them to me?"

"I'm gonna give you something," he murmured, low and sexy. "That's for damn sure."

I tossed back my head and laughed, loving the way I felt when he held me in his arms. When he looked at me with those gorgeous blue eyes. When he made me fall for him all over again with each passing day. Whether he was being funny or serious, his honesty still caused goosebumps to scamper up my arms. I often wondered if it had anything to do with the rainy night three years ago in that deserted parking lot. The night when he promised to always make me laugh and to give me extraordinary moments. Because since the night he tied himself to a tree for me, it had been one magical ride.

THE END

OTHER TITLES

For You Standalone Series
For Finlay (Book #1 Finlay & Caden's Story)
For Forester (Book #2 Trace's Story)
For Emery (Book #4 Grady's Story)

Savage Beasts Rock Star Standalone Series
Kozart
Treyton

Standalones
I Just Need You
You're the Reason
Until Alex
Since Drew
Before Hadley

ACKNOWLEDGEMENTS

Thank you so much for taking the time to read Sabrina and Crosby's story. I hope you enjoyed their relationship as much as I enjoyed writing it!

To all the bloggers and readers who have continued to spread the word about my books. No one would be reading my stories without your support. Thank you so very much!!!!

To my wonderful beta readers: Dali, Neilliza, Suzanne, Megan, Renee, Kim, Kerrie, Heather and Kat. Thank you for taking the time to read *For Crosby* (errors and all) and giving me your honest feedback. I am so fortunate to have all of you!

To my editor Stephanie Elliot. Thank you for always pushing me to be the best I can be—even if it means cutting lots of pages! Ha!

To Lindee Robinson for the beautiful cover photo. I can always count on you!

To Letitia at RBA Designs for creating another beautiful cover. Thank you for always being so amazing to work with!

And last, but certainly not least, to my husband and son. Thank you for your patience when I just need a few more minutes to finish a chapter. I could not do what I love doing without both of you being so understanding.

ABOUT THE AUTHOR

J. Nathan resides on the east coast with her husband and eight-year-old son. She is an avid reader of all things romance. Happy endings are a must. Alpha males with chips on their shoulders are an added bonus. When she's not curled up with a good book, she can be found spending time with family and friends and working on her next novel.

Made in the USA
Las Vegas, NV
17 May 2022